BLIND
PASS

ALSO BY BRADLEY WRIGHT

Tom Walker

Killer Instinct

Holy Water

Blind Pass

Deliverance

Alexander King

THE SECRET WEAPON

COLD WAR

MOST WANTED

POWER MOVE

ENEMY LINES

SMOKE SCREEN

SPY RING

Alexander King Prequels

WHISKEY & ROSES

VANQUISH

KING'S RANSOM

KING'S REIGN

SCOURGE

Lawson Raines

WHEN THE MAN COMES AROUND

SHOOTING STAR

Saint Nick

SAINT NICK

SAINT NICK 2

BLIND PASS

Copyright © 2023 by **Bradley Wright**
All rights reserved. No part of this publication may be reproduced, distributed or transmitted in any form or by any means, without prior written permission.
Bradley Wright/King's Ransom Publishing
www.bradleywrightauthor.com
Publisher's Note: This is a work of fiction. Names, characters, places, and incidents are a product of the author's imagination. Locales and public names are sometimes used for atmospheric purposes. Any resemblance to actual people, living or dead, or to businesses, companies, events, institutions, or locales is completely coincidental.
Blind Pass/Bradley Wright. -- 1st ed. ISBN - 9798870903880

*For Danny Meenach. A great farmer, and an even better family man.
You will be missed, but never forgotten.*

"If you want to see the sunshine, you have to weather the storm."

— FRANK LANE

BLIND PASS

PROLOGUE

St. Pete Beach, Florida

The bar at Sea Hags Bar & Grill was pitch black. As it would normally be on any morning at 3:30 am. However, now that the liquor bottles were missing from the bar that overlooked the marina, the tables and chairs were gone, and all that was left of the place were memories, it just felt different to Jonathan James. He'd frequented the place often before it closed last month. It had always been a lively joint. Good food, great live music, and enough drinks poured to make you not care if either of the first two things were true. For fifteen years it had been the place to be if you were located any where near the bridge on Blind Pass Rd that connected St. Pete Beach to the mainland.

Jon took another drag from his cigarette as he sat alone at the bar. Barely able to see a foot in front of him. The only visible light was beyond the marina. He could see through the windows behind the bar where a few of the condos and homes had their porch lights shining. The 7-Eleven a half mile down on the corner was still lit up too, even though it was closed. He took a drink of his black coffee he'd brought from his home that sat just on the other side of the intracoastal. His phone lit up. It was a text from the boat he was waiting for. Only five minutes out.

Sea Hags had another year on its lease when it closed. Jon didn't really like mixing business with pleasure, but the opportunity to have storage on the water that no one was going to care about for a year, that was a few hundred yards from his home on the water when he was staying in St. Pete was impossible to pass up. Added bonus was that his son lived close too. Not because he liked spending time with his degenerate son, but because Tate could keep an eye on his house for him when he was back in his more permanent home of Miami.

Though St. Pete Beach was a little on the sleepy side, this particular early morning, there was plenty of action. At least from his seat. Nothing got his adrenaline pumping like gun drops at 3:00 am. It had never been Jon's intention to get into the illegal trade of anything. But once he'd lost favor with the government officials who'd been throwing him the weapons contracts, his well-oiled machine came to a grinding halt. He still had all his contacts and information of a lot of other illegal buyers that he had refused over the years, so it was an easy transition. Though, this forced transaction wasn't one he wanted to be involved in at all, it still got the juices flowing.

His time in the military had taught him that war was going to be a part of humanity no matter what anyone did. There were either going to be people who challenge freedom, or crave it. And of course, even more important, it would always be a money making machine. One that had made him multi-millions after leaving the Army. And one that paid him even better after the *legit* government contracts dried up.

Criminals around the world existed in much greater numbers than countries. And they paid better too.

Jon ashed his cigarette on the beat up old wooden bar top and walked outside with the last of his coffee in hand. There was one orange light hanging from the roof, shining down on his man waiting on the dock. The water was calm on the intracoastal. The only sounds on the dock were the ropes groaning as the boats rocked in the water, and the seagulls fighting for their breakfast in the distance.

It was overcast above, so no light from the moon. Supposedly there was a major storm—possibly a hurricane on the way. Jon pulled out another cigarette and lit it with his Army-crested, Zippo lighter.

"Anything feels off, cover me and lets get the hell out of here," Jon said. His voice was gruff. Years of smoking had seemed to lower it about an octave, and added quite a bit of gravel.

"Yes sir," Mark said.

Mark Jansen had been Jon's number one for about six years. He went everywhere with him. Something about having a former Green Beret along was comforting when conversations happened with drug lords and warlords.

Jon was about to mention that the boat should be arriving any minute, but the buzzing sound he heard off to his right spoke for him. At Mark's feet were two large cases of various weapons. All of them high-powered and easy to shoot. A quarter of a million dollars worth. Not a large number. Certainly not by the standards that actually warranted Jon being there for the sale in person. He normally only showed up on the eight figure jobs. But this was a new buyer. And this had to go right for a lot more reasons than just selling guns. Anyway, he always wanted to know the competency level of his new business partners, and he could tell by the people the buyer sent on the first job whether or not they would be back for a second transaction.

"Your man ready?" Jon said.

"In position."

Jon learned very early on in the Army that underestimating, and/or under-preparing, was how people got themselves killed. He had Mark post a man in sniper position just in case the long shot scenario happened, and something crazy went down with the exchange. What he didn't like were the two men inside Sea Hags that weren't under his command. He would normally never have anyone around for a drop that wasn't part of his team, but this predicament his son had got him into left him without his normal level of control. The two men forced on him were wild cards. And wild cards can get you killed. Not something he liked being part of the night.

Mark touched his earpiece. "The boat is entering the marina. Stay sharp."

As the boat's motor drew closer, Jon caught the first glimpse of the light shining down over its bow. He looked over and gave Mark a nod. Mark returned it. There were about eight rows of boats sitting out in front of him. About ten in each row. Not a large marina. The boat made its turn back toward Sea Hags, and the yellow light was pointed straight at them.

That was the first time Jon saw something move in the space between the water and the dock on his left. It could have been a manatee. They were known to frequent the marina. Jon took a step closer to get a better look, but couldn't see anything this time. He didn't like the feel of the entire situation, so he placed his hand on his pistol at the small of his back and walked over behind Mark. Ready, but not wanting to show he was holding a weapon.

The boat pulled up, the engine near idle, and the stern

swung toward the dock. Jon looked over and nodded to Mark who then stepped over and caught the rope thrown from the back of the boat. Jon watched Mark tie the rope to the cleat as Mark watched the man who'd tossed the rope.

"Let's make this quick," a voice from the boat said. Then a large man stepped into the yellow light glowing from Sea Hags.

Jon looked down at the man's hands. He was holding a large duffel bag.

"Quick works for me," Jon said. Jon nodded to Mark. Mark moved over and picked up one of the cases of weapons. "You can set the bag right there for me, and open it up," Jon said. He pointed off to his left.

The man holding the bag just tossed it onto the dock. "You need to count it, count it."

Jon stepped back so Mark could get through. "Trust is earned, not given."

The big guy took the weapons cases one by one from Mark and handed them off to the man who had tossed the rope a moment ago. Jon caught a glimpse behind both men and there was a woman there. It was just a flash of her but he could see the light shine off of her golden hair. The smaller man who'd thrown the rope opened up the first case and began checking it with a flashlight. Mark had already taken the duffle bag and set it down beside Sea Hags. The big man on the boat leaned down and picked up one more bag.

That's when the sirens sounded. Reflex made Jon reach for his pistol, but he knew he couldn't pull it. If this was a sting, he couldn't go shooting federal agents. That wouldn't be worth the punishment under any circumstance. But that's when the two men that weren't part of his team—that he was afraid would be a problem if something went down—began firing at the boat from inside Sea Hags. Jon felt Mark grab him and pull him down behind a storage container that separated them from the boat in case the people on the boat decided to return fire.

"Get this boat out of here!" the big man shouted as he reached down and cut the rope that tethered them to the dock.

"Hold your fire!" Mark shouted into his earpiece as he dove for cover behind the metal storage container, letting his sniper know that he wasn't to shoot. He knew the consequences of killing an agent the same as Jon did. "Disappear!"

Just as Jon landed behind the storage container on top of Mark, he saw the big man dive out of the light, back into the boat, as its engine fired up. Jon heard more gunfire from behind him over the sirens. Then he noticed two men swim out from under the dock. They hadn't been manatees. Jon had been setup. And as soon as they made their presence known, the two thugs forced on Jon turned their guns on them and shot both of them down.

"No!" Jon shouted. "Stop shooting!"

The boat's bow swerved left as it began to pull away. Mark held Jon in place even though he kept shouting for the men who weren't team members to stop shooting.

The gunshots stopped and Jon heard one of the men behind him shout in his Mexican accent. "Get the boat. We're going after them!"

Jon had Mark position a boat one row over and out toward the end of the ramp, ready to move as a backup plan. The two cartel thugs must have heard Mark and Jon discussing it, because he watched as they ran across the dock and jumped on it. Jon would have loved for himself and Mark to turn their guns on the two of them, but he couldn't shoot made men. The repercussions of those two dying because of Jon and his operation would make the already horrible situation he was stuck in, far worse. The cartel didn't like their men to come up dead. But he didn't want them to hurt the people who were making the drop from the boat that just pulled away either. The people on the boat must be federal agents too. Jon didn't want to get blamed for their deaths because of what two men did that he never even wanted around.

When Jon jumped to his feet to go after the boat, it began to pull away. He wasn't going to make it. But that's when a man came bounding out of Sea Hags that he had never expected to see.

Jon raised his gun. "Walker?"

CHAPTER ONE

The bright golden blaze that had been shining just beyond the deck rail had slowly transitioned to orange and pink hues as the sun dropped steadily toward the waters of the Gulf of Mexico. A couple of seagulls floated in front of the horizon, making a great picture for all the watchers who were into pictures. Tom Walker wasn't one of those people. He wasn't sure he'd ever even used the camera feature on his phone. It was one of the many trivial thoughts he'd pondered in the hour or so he'd been sitting at his high top table overlooking the beach from the second story of a bar and restaurant called Caddy's. Walker wasn't aware before he'd walked over from his condo, but Caddy's was apparently the most popular spot on that particular section of Treasure Island, Florida. Which was just across the bridge from St. Pete Beach where he was staying.

Most of the partying was going on down below on the first level and spilling out onto the beach. That's where the live music was playing, and therefore where the younger in the crowd had gathered. The place was painted in all the neon beachy colors. They had picnic tables out on the sand that gave way to umbrella-covered chairs where people could get serious about their skin cancer. Walker had never been a fan of the beach. He preferred his meals and drinks void of chewing sand. The rashes of the salt water had never been a love of his either. Though he'd never actually had one. Slowing down to take in sunsets hadn't been in his life plan when he'd been murdering bad guys.

There was a full bar behind him, and the beach was far enough below so the sand stayed away. The music was an island vibe, mixed with tributes to some of the favorites from decades' passed. There was a couple of families sitting and eating off to his right on the uncovered portion of the deck. He and only one other person were covered. And she looked even more disinterested in what was going on than Walker was. She hadn't much looked up from her laptop long enough to see the waitress go by.

Walker enjoyed people watching. Watching people had inadvertently been his life's work . . . well . . . before he would jab them with a knife, or spread their brains across wherever they happened to be at the moment. So, watching with a bourbon in his plastic cup (no glass near the beach) was a nice, nonviolent change.

He was in desperate need of this nonviolent change too. A week ago, his skills as a trained killer had been on full display. The lake town of Soddy Daisy had turned out to be anything but the getaway he'd hoped for. So far, Florida was working out better. But it had only been a few days. However, as the warm sea breeze blew across his table, he was happy with where things were at the moment.

The woman with her nose buried in her laptop walked by and leaned on the wooden rail as she looked out at the ocean. She turned and looked at Walker. "I bet they don't get a lot of people who come here and sip bourbon, neat, right out of their fancy plastic cups."

Walker looked down. He was sure she was right. It wasn't his favorite vehicle for his whiskey. But he was anything but pretentious, so he didn't mind.

"Yeah?" he winked. "I'm sure you're right. Probably not a lot of patrons come here and stick their nose in a laptop for hours on end either."

She glanced back at her table. The laptop was still open.

"Probably not," she admitted with a smile.

Her black pencil skirt hugged her curves. She had a white and black striped button-down shirt still tucked into it. The sleeves were rolled up and her collar was open enough to keep her from looking stuffy. Her long, straight blond hair was blowing in the breeze. She was stunning.

Walker said, "Now that we know we've noticed each other, can I buy you a drink? You can still work on your laptop. I just didn't want to end our little exchange awkwardly."

She smiled.

He smiled.

"Awkward on purpose, to avoid being awkward," she said. "Interesting approach."

"I was going to go with something about it being because your beautiful eyes matched the emerald green water just behind you, but it's a little early in the evening for cheesy pick-up lines. True as it may be."

Walker felt he was doing a good job exuding confidence, but in reality, he hadn't spoken with a woman in such a way in a very long time.

"That would've worked too. I'm a sucker for lonely men who are good at filling out their v-neck t-shirts."

Walker laughed. "Does that mean you aren't all work and no play?"

"Probably not, but I am certainly spent for today's work allocation."

Walker stood from his chair, stepped around the table, and extended his hand. "Tom Walker," he said, immediately having to hide the fact that he was upset with himself. Sixty seconds in the presence of a beautiful woman and he'd already forgotten his new identity was *David* Walker, to conceal the fact that he was Tom.

"Friends call me Walker," he added just as she was about to speak.

She stepped forward. "All right, Walker." She shook his hand. "Taylor Crenshaw. My friends don't call me much anymore. I've become a bit of a workaholic."

"I know a little bit about work overtaking your life myself."

The band below them switched gears and a steel drum version of *Summer Breeze* by Seals & Croft tickled Taylor's ears. She closed her eyes and her hips began to sway. "I love this song."

Walker did too, but mostly because of the affect it had on Taylor. She was borderline mesmerizing.

"This song feels like a margarita," Walker said. "Objections?"

Taylor opened her eyes. "Sounds perfect, actually. No salt please."

"I'll be right back."

She mouthed the words *thank you* as Walker stepped away. He felt an odd sensation as he moved toward the bar. Something like his nerve endings had just caught fire. He looked back at the rail toward the ocean where Taylor was dancing. The feeling intensified. That was a first.

He somehow made it to the bar without tripping over himself. A real feat for someone as intoxicated by beauty as he'd seemed to be. He tore his gaze from Taylor and found the young bartender smiling at him. His name tag said Adam.

"Two margaritas. Rocks, not salt."

"You got it," Adam said. Then immediately got to work on the drinks. "She's special, isn't she?" he said.

Walker glanced back over, Taylor turned and flashed him a smile.

"She's . . . something," Walker managed.

"You must be all right yourself," Adam said.

"How do you mean?"

He began shaking the margaritas. "This is her fourth night in a row here. I've seen a few guys try, but she hardly even looks up from her laptop."

Walker laid a fifty on the bar. "She must have felt sorry for the man without a friend."

Adam poured the margaritas garnished with a lime into the Caddy's themed neon plastic cups. Then he smiled as he pushed them over. "The humble approach," he said. "I gotta try that one."

Walker winked. He didn't know why he winked. Maybe it was because the kid was trying to have a bro moment with him. And Walker doesn't really have bro moments. But what the kid didn't know was that regardless of what Walker thought of himself, humble wasn't an approach, it was a lifestyle.

"Keep the change," Walker said as he turned back to Taylor, margaritas in hand.

The band had just moved on to Billy Joel so Taylor was walking his way.

She took a margarita from his hand. "Thank you. I'll get the next round." Then she turned and walked back to his table by the rail. She sat facing the sunset, he took the seat beside her. She raised her cup. "Cheers."

Walker raised his.

Taylor smiled. "May we get what we want. May we get what we need. But may we never get what we deserve." Then she touched his cup with hers as she laughed.

"Cheers to that," Walker said. They both took a sip. Walker recognized the toast. "Does that mean you have some Irish in you?"

"My mother," Taylor said. "She was a Fitzpatrick." She touched her lips. "This is delicious. Haven't had one in a while."

"All work and no play as they say."

Taylor shrugged. The light of the setting sun gleaned in her eyes. "Speaking of work, what do you do? You're a little above the partying age, but quite a bit below the average age of the snow birds who migrate down here."

"I am no snowbird, but I am retired."

Taylor looked impressed. "I would ask you if you were some sort of tech millionaire or something, but your build, your ever-so-slight southern drawl, and that pistol you have concealed on your hip there certainly say otherwise."

Now it was Walker who looked impressed.

Taylor smiled and raised an eyebrow. "Part of my job is to notice things . . . everything, really."

Walker smiled, then looked back over at her laptop that was sitting on the table. "By notice things, you mean, like, how for the last hour you haven't entered one thing on that spreadsheet you have pulled up on your computer? Or how you've only ordered soda water with a lime? Or maybe that your shoulder holster that you kept in the car left a wrinkle patch on both shoulders of your blouse there?"

Taylor took a drink of her margarita. Now her look was more of a subtle, "whoah". "Okay . . . that was impressive. Dare I say we are in a similar line of work?"

"I would say not," Walker said. "But both do involve guns." He drank. "CIA or FBI?"

"You tell me since you seem to know it all," she said.

"FBI. And judging by what Adam back there behind the bar says, your waiting for someone in particular to come to this place. Otherwise you would never waste four nights in a row."

Impressed again, she nodded. "How do you know I wasn't waiting for you?"

Walker took his shot. "Because I'm not involved in whatever crime you happen to be investigating. You just approached me because you couldn't sit at that table any longer and you hoped I wasn't too much of a meat-head to carry on a decent conversation . . . which you haven't had with a man in quite some time."

Taylor looked comically offended. Like it didn't really hurt her feelings, but maybe there was a ring of truth in there.

Walker smiled. "And might I add, if that last wild guess I just took is true, that is the real crime you should be investigating."

Taylor smiled. "You're like, the most un-charming, charming guy I've ever met."

They shared a laugh. Then they imbibed in a couple more drinks as day became night. It was one of the best evenings Walker'd had in a really, really long time.

CHAPTER TWO

Walker rolled over and picked up his phone from the nightstand. 5:00 am. Though he'd had more alcohol than usual last night by the beach with Taylor, his body was too fixed to his schedule to ever let him sleep anything off. Luckily for him, he'd always had a high tolerance when it came to alcohol. But even then, he could still tell he'd let loose a bit. It had been a long time since his first thought when he woke up in the morning was of a woman. Maybe it was the first time. His was a strange existence—being as old as he is without ever falling in love and he knew it. Not that he was in love, but he had sure loved spending time with Taylor. Regardless, it was certainly better than waking with thoughts of murder and mayhem.

Her eyes were what had really pulled him in. They smiled every time her mouth smiled. As if she had genuinely been enjoying herself. Walker knew he sure did. He let out a sigh and rolled to a seated position. He ran his fingers through his hair, then got up and pulled back the curtains. Still dark as night. The north facing side of the condo looked across the community pool on the other side of the parking lot, nine floors down. Beyond it lay the peaceful intracoastal waters. The homes which surrounded the water reflected their white and yellow dock and patio lights. The sunrise off to the East was going to be gorgeous.

He walked out of the bedroom into the living area. The condo he was staying in had been renovated not long ago. Walker was no interior designer, but he felt the owners had done a good job balancing modern and beach house decor. The room was open to the kitchen, and he walked past the round dining room table to open the curtains facing West. Just beyond the marina, a few restaurants, and some residences, the Gulf of Mexico stretched into the distance. Though he couldn't see it in the current darkness of 5:00am.

Walker moved to the kitchen and touched start on the coffee machine. The gym at the Yacht and Tennis Club where he was staying didn't open until six, but TW, the man he was renting from finagled Walker a key so he could get in early. He'd only been there four days, but he'd already established a routine. Workout in his swimming trunks in the gym, then laps in the pool, then coffee. It was working well thus far and he was beginning to settle into the place.

Walker was young for the three-tower condominium complex. The few people that did stay year-round were mostly well into retirement. Everyone so far had been nice enough. As one would expect from the people wealthy enough to spend their golden years in a beautiful place like St. Pete Beach. Life was slow here. Walker liked that. He had yet to venture out to try to find someone to help out of an unfortunate situation—his newfound passion in life. And now that he'd met Taylor, maybe he would just let something come to him. He was going to meet her at Caddy's again that evening. He was excited about that. Helping others with his *killer* skills could wait a little longer.

Walker changed clothes and made it through his workout. Today was leg day. He hated leg day. The pool had been warm when he'd went in for his laps. His legs were pretty dead, so his arms had to pull more of the load. He was feeling that when he poured himself a cup of coffee. The sun beyond the window was on the rise. Walker's phone began vibrating.

Tim Lawson.

"What do ya say, old man?" Walker answered.

Tim had been checking in regularly since Walker left Soddy Daisy, Tennessee. Tim was in Laguna Hills, California visiting his son's family.

"Not much buddy. I'm livin' the life here."

"Yeah? You must be if you're already awake. What is it, four o'clock there?"

"Sleep is for the weak," Tim said.

"Yeah? That, or the well rested."

"Ain't that right. How's the beach treatin' you?"

Walker opened the sliding glass door to the deck. He took his coffee over to the table at the corner. From there he could look left and see the Gulf, and right to see the intracoastal.. "Damn fine I don't mind saying."

"That's good. You sound relaxed."

Walker took a deep inhale of the sea breeze wafting up to him. "Yes sir. Pretty relaxed. How's Chris and the family?"

"Good as ever. He's already up on a conference call to some other country. Girls are glad to have pops here and his wife Jen is a damn fine cook. I'm spoiled rotten at this point."

"Love to hear it," Walker said.

"Anything exciting happen yet?"

Walker's mind jumped to Taylor dancing in her tight skirt last night. "Not really."

"No? None of the snowbird ladies tried to cook you dinner yet?"

Walker laughed. "They are very sweet. I will say that. Met a nice woman last night at a beach bar."

"There you go. You didn't blow it did you?"

"I think I did all right."

"Good. If you like her, let her know. Life is short buddy. Make big deals out of little things."

"I'm seeing her again tonight."

"That's what I'm talkin' about. Good for you. You deserve it. Soak it up."

Walker took a sip of coffee. He decided right then to absolutely take Tim's advice on the matter.

"What's next for you, Tim?"

"Eh, I got some work to do on the farm when I get back after next week. I'm gonna build me on something new to the house."

"Sounds expensive," Walker said.

"Life always is. Speaking of, it's none of my business, but since you don't work anymore, you good on money?"

"I'm set."

"Good. What about what you'd talked about. You gonna look into finding someone to help?"

"That's the goal."

"Well, since you've met you a lady, why don't you take the time to help yourself for a little bit?"

"I think I might. Trouble has a way of finding me anyway. I'm sure something will pop up."

"All right, buddy. I'm going to have some coffee with my boy. Holler at me soon. I want the details on the girl."

"Will do. Thanks for calling, Tim. Talk soon."

Walker ended the call and closed his eyes. The warm breeze carried the calls of some seagulls fighting over a meal. The buzz of a couple of boats out in the intracoastal too. It was something Walker thought he might be able to get used to. All the years in between jobs, he never really understood how much the stress of waiting on the next call for the next kill weighed on him. Now that he felt so weightless, it was very apparent.

Walker's stomach growled. It was time for a fill up. There was a restaurant just across the short bridge that he could walk to. Breakfast, then a little time at the gun range sounded like a plan. He didn't have anything else to do. Might as well stay sharp. If he'd learned anything about himself, anytime he felt at peace, something always came along to shatter that state of being. He wanted to be ready when it did. No matter how long it took to find him.

CHAPTER THREE

"It must happen now," Javier Vasquez said in a stern voice. "I don't care if you say you are not a drug dealer. You are now. And Miami is someone else's territory, so find a new place to sell."

Jonathan James cleared his throat as his blood pressure rose. But he took a deep breath and calmed himself. There were very few people in the world Jon would let speak to him like that, let alone demand things of him. But when the Jaurez Cartel leader has you by the balls, Vasquez was one of the few that Jon had no choice but to roll over for.

"Remember, Señor James, it isn't me who let his son botch a twenty million dollar arms deal. But it is you who is now responsible for paying me back."

"I can pay you back without selling drugs. It will take a little time, but I'll get it done."

Vasquez was quiet.

Jon had known when his son, Tate, had let another cartel intercept his weapon delivery to the Jaurez Cartel it meant big trouble. Add on to that where he also managed to let the money get taken in the exchange, *and* the drug shipment

Vasquez's men were trying to piggyback after Jon's weapons deal? Yeah, there would be consequences, and they would come swiftly. Jon tried to bury the fact that the opposing cartel learned about the exchange because of Tate's interaction with a woman from that opposing cartel the night before, but one of Vasquez's men had found out. Vasquez made Jon promise he would make it right, or his son Tate would die. Now here Jon was, having to listen to a mouthy cartel leader demand things Jon had never wanted to be a part of.

However, this day was a long time coming. Jon knew it. The minute his government weapons contracts were terminated and he made the decision to keep supplying whoever would be willing to buy, it had just been a matter of time. You run with dogs, you catch fleas. And these fleas were going to have one hell of a bite.

"Mr. James," Vasquez finally spoke. This time his voice was devoid of emotion. "Do us both a favor and stop acting like you have a choice in the matter. You will do this. And you will stop making me have to tell you so. Do we understand?"

Jon walked outside his open sliding glass doors onto the pool deck. The intracoastal waters shimmered just beyond the dock where he kept his boat. He let out a deep sigh. "I understand."

"Tell me where you want the shipment and I'll have it to you by tomorrow night."

Vasquez ended the call.

Jon looked at his phone, then tossed it as hard as he could. It landed in the water just beyond his boat. He was furious. Furious at his son for botching the deal and putting them in debt to a cartel leader, but even more angry at himself for letting Tate run such an important transaction. Jon knew his son wasn't ready. But he had grown tired of Tate begging for more of a role. It had been a terrible time to see if Tate could sink or swim, with such a powerful and ruthless criminal on the other end of the deal. And Tate had sunk like a torpedo in the side of a kayak.

Jon walked back inside and powered on his spare burner phone. He dialed his son's number.

Tate picked up on the fifth ring. "Hello?" His voice sounded tired and sleepy.

"Are you still in bed?" Jon said.

"Yeah, why? It's only 9:00 am."

Jon took the phone away from his ear. He could feel every muscle in his body tense. His jaw was clenched and his grip on the phone was about to break it in half. He took a deep breath. Then another. Then put the phone back to his ear. "You're out."

Those words had been floating in Jon's mind for months. He'd practically been dreaming of the day he could say them. Today was the day he could no longer tolerate his spoiled, unappreciative, half-wit son.

"Out of what?"

Jon went numb. His shoulder's relaxed as if someone had pulled the weight of a grizzly bear off of them. "Don't call me. You can stay in the place in Miami until I clean your mess up here. Two weeks. Then you're out of there too."

"What? Dad! I can fix this. I told you I would fix this!"

"You can't even fix your hair without help," Jon said.

"I'm going to fix it. You'll see. Then it will be okay!"

"Stay out of it. That's final. Good luck, son."

"I'm going to fix it!"

Jon ended the call. He would have tossed that phone in the ocean too if it weren't his last burner. He didn't know whether it was his fault, or Tate's mother. Both he guessed. Jon was gone too much, and his mother was way too soft on Tate. A kid disaster scenario. The only way Tate was going to make something of himself is if he could somehow fail, then pick himself back up. Jon wasn't going to hold his breath.

What he was going to do, however, was get himself away from Javier Vasquez and the Juarez Cartel. Whatever it took. He had absolutely no network setup for drug dealing. And he wasn't about to start. His line of work had him fostering relationships with shady people, so he just had to hope that one of a few phone calls could lead him to someone who did have that network. Then he could sell the drugs that Vasquez was making him unload in bulk. He would just have to make up the difference with his own hard-earned money. Perks of having a degenerate son he supposed.

Jon walked back inside. The photo of his late wife, Madeline, was staring at him from the corner of the fireplace mantle. Though she was smiling, he knew she would be disappointed in him. But she wasn't the one left having to deal with Tate and his never grow up—Peter Pan syndrome. Maddie had been gone for almost a decade, but her piercing blue eyes still had the ability to absolutely melt him. Her last words to Jon before the cancer took her were, "take care of him". Jon knew what she meant. However, he also understood that the only way to truly help his son now was to let him find his way on his own. Any more than that, and Tate would never grow up.

Jon went over to his briefcase and pulled out his address book. Tate made fun of him a lot for keeping paper records. But Tate also had no idea how to keep things private in 2023. Jon flipped through the pages and found his old Army buddy's contact. Bud Scarberry. They'd spent most of Jon's fifteen years of service together. When Jon got his first government contract to deal arms, Bud went left and took on work as a mercenary. They'd tried to keep up with each other, but life kept pulling them apart. Like Jon, Bud's work brought him in contact with a wide array of characters—

many of them criminals. It was the best place Jon knew to start. Hopefully someone in Bud's past had some drug dealing in their repertoire. Or at least knew of someone who did. They would be getting one hell of a deal for what Jon had to sell. He could only hope that would be enough.

Jon went to his burner, typed in Bud's number, then texted their age-old SOS code: 2769 (ARMY). Bud would know it was Jon reaching out. How long it would take him to reply would be the kicker. Because time was not on Jon's side.

CHAPTER FOUR

CADDY'S WAS HOPPING ONCE AGAIN. BOB MARLEY'S *No Woman No Cry* was the chosen song of the live band. Walker stepped past the hostess and about six other people to get around to the stairs that lead to the upper deck. As he ascended, his stomach began acting funny. Not sick funny. Not really hungry funny either. This was more of a butterfly sort of feeling. One he both enjoyed, and didn't like at all. He didn't know why he had trouble leaning into his feelings. Especially about women. But he had never been good at it. And that was apparent as he scolded himself for feeling anything for a stranger at all.

Then he saw her.

Taylor stood out like a single golden light bulb on a green Christmas tree. He walked down the deck toward her. She was at the same table just in front of the bar as she had been the night before. Walker scolded himself once again as he smelled his own scent. Actually, it was his landlord TW's scent. Walker never wore cologne, but before he left to walk to Caddy's, Tim texted him: *Now don't you leave for your date without smelling good. Women love that shit.* After about ten minutes of back and forth with himself, he picked up a bottle of Guerlain that TW had in his bathroom closet. It smelled fine, but he felt like an imposter. A sham for wearing the cologne, and also for letting Tim talk him into it.

That imposter feeling, and every other thing going on in Walker's mind quickly faded when Taylor noticed him coming toward her. Her smile was wide as she jumped up from her seat. She wrapped him up in a hug like they'd known each other forever.

"Mmm," she moaned. "You smell good."

Thanks Tim. Thanks TW.

"Then we are a good pair, because you look fantastic."

Taylor had ditched the FBI get up for a white sundress. Her tan skin glowed beneath it.

"Why thank you, Mr. Walker."

He noticed there was no laptop on her table as well. No drink either.

"Thirsty?" Walker said.

"Thought you'd never ask."

"What are you feeling?"

"How bout a Riesling?" Taylor scrunched her nose. "Not sure this is the type of place that has that, but I thought it would look good next to your bourbon neat. You know, all sophisticated of us."

Walker smiled. "I'm sure they'll have something like it if I'm allowed to substitute?"

"By all means."

"Be right back."

Taylor squeezed his hand as she took a seat. Walker turned toward the bar and there was Adam, Walker's favorite bartender, just smiling away. Walker stepped up to the bar and shrugged. Adam held out his fist. Walker gave it a bump with his.

"My man," Adam said with a laugh. "I knew you were going to pull it off."

"Not sure I've pulled anything off yet, Adam. But at least she hasn't told me to get lost."

"Right. The humble approach. I love it."

Walker smiled and shook his head. "Bourbon neat. And a Riesling for the lady if you have it."

"We've got it. Bourbon preference? I know we don't really have any top shelf here for you, Mr. Kentucky."

"Maker's is fine."

"You got it."

Adam stepped away to pour the drinks. He seemed like a good kid. Couldn't have been much older than twenty-one. Walker glanced back at Taylor just as she was running her fingers through her hair. Then twirling it at the end. Walker read somewhere that if a woman touched you at all during a conversation, she liked you, because she would never touch you otherwise. He'd already received a hug and a hand squeeze, so he was going to take the pressure off himself and just enjoy getting to know her.

Walker laid cash on the bar as Adam set down the drinks.

"Old school," Adam said as he picked up the fifty. "I like it. Just wave at me when you want another round. Have fun."

"Thanks Adam."

"Thank you!"

Adam moved on to the next eager drinker as Walker stepped back over to Taylor and took a seat. He slid the Riesling over to her.

"They had it?"

"Yes ma'am."

"We really class this place up, don't we?" Taylor said with a laugh.

"High society for sure."

Walker looked beyond the covered portion of the deck

out toward the ocean. The clouds were a little thicker than last night. The band was playing *Every Breath You Take* by The Police.

"This your theme song?" Walker said, smiling.

Taylor nearly spit out her wine. She laughed until the singer down below said Sting's line, "I'll be watching you."

"You know, the FBI actually does a lot more than just *watch* people."

Walker scrunched his nose and cocked his head sideways. "But do they?"

"Eventually, yes. And what about you, Mr. Comedian? Didn't you do the same thing as me? How much different could it have been?"

Miles and miles of difference.

"I think probably a little different," Walker said.

"So we're not really going to get to know each other then? Just flirt and keep it surface?"

Walker took a sip of his bourbon. "I don't really have a lot to tell."

"I can tell that's bullshit," Taylor said. "But that's fine. Not pressuring you. Just wanted to make sure we are on the same page. I'm not really a fling kind of girl. No matter how cute you look in those jeans."

"You should see me without them."

Walker wasn't sure where that line came from. He was normally the self deprecating type. Especially after he was just told by Taylor that she was basically a no-fly zone. He was just passing through. She knew that. Wasn't telling him she wasn't a fling type of girl pretty much pumping the brakes?

"Cute probably wouldn't be the word I would use for that, I'm sure," she flirted back.

That was a good sign, right? Walker was terrible at this. So much so that many times he'd avoided a lot of potentially fun situations like this one just so he wouldn't have to play the game.

Walker took a breath and sat back in his seat. He allowed himself to enjoy the moment. His life hadn't been filled with many good ones, so he was trying to get better at soaking in the ones that did come along. He knew he was supposed to be enjoying the sunset view, but he really couldn't stop looking at Taylor. She was like a sunset all to herself. Captivating.

Then Taylor's posture shifted. Not in the way one might shift to sit on a different leg, but she stiffened. Like something she didn't like just grabbed her attention. Walker followed her eyes to the deck rail. There was a man standing there, alone, taking in the view. He seemed to be a few years younger than Walker. Long brown hair pulled into a ponytail. His shirt looked like one of those ultra expensive silk Versace shirts with the crazy gold pattern. The only reason Walker recognized it was because a couple of his previous targets had money to burn, and absolutely no sense of style. Not that Walker had that sense, but ugly was ugly.

Walker looked back at Taylor. "Everything all right?"

Taylor whipped her head around as if she'd been caught doing something wrong. "What?" She glanced back toward the man at the rail. "Sure. Yeah, I'm fine."

"Don't they teach you how to lie better than that at the Bureau?"

She didn't know what to say.

"It's fine," Walker said. "I'm just giving you a hard time."

"Yeah," she shook her head as if shaking from a trance. "No, I know. Sorry. I . . ."

She looked back at the man.

"He the one you've been looking for?"

Another surprised look. Then she took a breath. "I forgot, you can probably read all of this all over me, right?"

Walker smiled. "Pretty sure anyone could."

"That bad, huh?"

"If you need to do something, believe me, no one understands more than I do."

"No, it's fine. We're fine. I was just caught a little off guard."

"This isn't an ex thing, right? This is a mark?"

Taylor laughed. "Ex? God no. Yes, he is a mark. But I don't really need anything out of it, I was just here surveilling. Seeing who he speaks to, and so forth. This doesn't have to interrupt our evening."

Her sea-foam green eyes lingered to let him know she was sincere.

"Could also make it fun. I was always solo. Never staked anything out with a partner before."

Tayler smiled. "That what we are?"

Walker laughed. "For now." He picked up his glass, held it up, and waited for her to clink his. "To our first stake out."

Taylor laughed. "Our first stake out." He could see the tension fall from her shoulders. At least he'd done something right.

"You, of course, don't have to tell me anything," Walker said. "I can make it up."

"Sounds like something Internal Affairs might say."

"I can assure you, I was never paid to catch my own team up in a mistake. Like I said, I've never even had a team."

"Black Ops then?" she said.

"Something like that."

Taylor took a sip of her wine. "This is Tate James. Son of Jonathan James. Jon used to be an arms dealer contracted by the US government. He's believed to still be dealing arms, but now without contracts. His son here, is more just a way in. He's your typical spoiled brat. Entitled to everything even though he's earned nothing. We think a deal went bad with a cartel in Mexico, but we're trying to piece together Tate's involvement. That, and the red flag that got us here is that on the side, he's been scamming people at the Yacht & Tennis Club back behind us.

"That's where I'm staying. Scamming?"

"Scamming, maybe worse. Property value in the condos has skyrocketed recently. We think that Tate here, and some of his men, are bullying people who own condos that need remodeling. He buys them at unrealistically cheap prices, then flips them after fixing them up."

"That doesn't really sound like a Federal problem," Walker said. "So I'm assuming you want him to get to his dad."

"Right. Or the cartel they're dealing with. That's the even bigger whale. I was tying to observe him here because we know he comes here quite a bit. Brings girls. Tries to show off in front of his men. Often meets other sinister characters and so forth. Just want a full view of who he's working with."

"Got it."

Three men walked up and shook hands with Tate as Walker and Taylor watched on. They seemed to be newer acquaintances, judging by the formal nature of the greeting. Tate walked them over to a long table to the left of Walker. He immediately proved what Taylor had said when he shouted to Adam behind the bar, demanding he hurry up and take their drink order. When Walker turned to look at Adam, he could see tension in him that hadn't been there before.

"See how he keeps messing with his nose?" Taylor said.

Tate rubbed his nose, squeezed it, then rubbed it again.

"Cocaine. Yeah. I was trained to see who is tweaking too. Pretty important when lives are on the line."

Taylor gave him the side-eye.

A couple of women walked up and made their way to

Tate's table. The first walked around and gave Tate an uncomfortably intimate kiss that lingered far longer than it should've. Walker and Taylor shared a glance. Smiling between each other. Then the woman finally pulled away and introduced her friends to the group. Tate's chest puffed out even farther.

"Hey bartender! What the hell man? You don't like business? Drinks. Now."

Walker looked back at Adam—now he looked frightened. Walker didn't like it. He started to get up. Then he felt Taylor grab his wrist.

"Don't," she said. "It's not safe."

Walker stayed up for a moment. Until Tate's eyes met his.

"You got a problem, asshole?" Tate said.

Walker didn't reply. He felt Taylor pull at him. Slowly, he sat back down in his seat.

"I didn't think so," Tate said, mocking him.

"Let it go, Walker," Taylor said. "Those men he's with, they're dangerous."

"You know them?"

"Local gang. Drug dealers, guns, and probably some worse things. Small-time now, but growing. More of what we would like to know."

Walker nodded. He took a breath, letting the steam he was feeling out.

Taylor moved her hand from his wrist to holding his hand. "I'm sorry. I should have had us meet somewhere else. We can leave."

Walker looked over at her. Grinned. "It's fine." Then he looked back at Adam who was frantically trying to ready some drinks. It was clear that Adam knew who these men were as well, and he was scared of them.

"You can't leave now, can you?" Taylor said as she too glanced back at Adam.

"Don't think so. That okay?"

Taylor squeezed his hand. "We'll play the cards we're dealt." Then she winked.

There was a lot going on in Walker's mind at the moment. But one of the things that was shining through, almost as bright as Taylor's smile, was the feeling he couldn't shake that he just might have already found that trouble that he knew was going to eventually find him.

CHAPTER FIVE

Walker was forced to temper that ingrained killer instinct that wasn't often easy to control. He and Taylor had tried to get to know each other over the next hour as the sun faded into oblivion, but it was difficult with the Tate show going on just a table away. He was loud and obnoxious, the women he was with were loud and obnoxious, and the more they drank, the more the men who met them there began to match Tate's energy.

Taylor tried to lighten the mood with surprise tequila shots that she'd brought up from her trip to the ladies room. And with another full round down between them, it was definitely taking the edge off. But the way Tate increasingly degraded Adam was becoming harder to watch. Even for Taylor. But she was the calm in the storm, assuring Walker that when they left they could leave a little extra for Adam's tip to make his night a little better.

Then the server showed up with a tray of food.

Tate stood up after his plate was set in front of him. "What the hell is this shit?" he shouted.

The waitress, who wasn't much older than Adam, coward backward. "I'm sorry, sir. Is there something wrong with it?"

Tate reached down and picked up his plate. "Is there something wrong with it? Are you serious? Did you look at this slop? You telling me this is okay to serve?"

The waitress took a step back. "I-I'm really sorry, sir."

"No," Tate pressed. "Did you actually look at this before you brought it up here?"

"I—no, sir."

Then he reached for her arm. Walker stood immediately as if it were a reflex. Because for him, it was. He'd watched a woman get manhandled too many times in his life to standby and watch again. This time, Taylor didn't catch his wrist.

Tate pulled the waitress toward him. "Well look at it. Closer!" He moved his hand up to behind her head. Then he began to push her head down toward the plate. "Does that look edible to you?"

The women at the table were laughing. The rest of the men were too. Walker's adrenaline began to leak into his system.

Adam went running by on his left. "Let go of her! You can't touch her like that!"

"Please don't," Taylor said. "I already texted to have a unit come to the restaurant. I don't want you to get hurt."

Tate let go of the waitress. She almost fell backward by how quickly he released her. "I can touch who I want, when I want. You think you can stop me?"

Now one of the other men at the table stood up and stared down at Adam. A bouncer came jogging in from the right side of the deck. "What the hell is going on here?"

"Just let them handle it, Walker," Taylor said, gently placing her hand on his wrist again.

The man looking at Adam turned, and before the bouncer even knew what was coming, the man reached back and threw a hard right cross, knocking the bouncer off his feet. Then he turned and grabbed Adam by the shirt.

Walker looked down at Taylor. Not that he needed permission, but he really didn't want to make life harder for her. However, he couldn't sit and watch these thugs do anything to Adam. Taylor didn't say anything, but she did let go of his arm.

Walker looked back to the man holding onto Adam. "Let him go."

As if the preverbal record scratched, everyone stopped and looked over at Walker. The people sitting at nearby tables began to back away as they watched.

"The hell did you just say?" Tate said.

"The police are on their way," Walker said, doing everything he could to not just go over and run right through every one of these men. "If this stops right now, I'm sure it can be chalked up to a little too much to drink."

"That right?" Tate said as he stepped around the waitress. "You think because you're a big man that you can do something?"

"I'm not trying to do anything but warn you that the cops are coming. If you leave now, I'm sure this will blow over."

Tate stepped around the last chair. No more than twenty feet from Walker now. The red hair that was pulled into a ponytail behind his head bounced as he stepped. He began to rub his scraggly beard as he eyed Walker. "You serious right now? You really call the cops on us?"

Walker didn't speak.

"You have no idea who we are do you?"

This was getting harder for Walker. Tate was clearly one of those men who'd never really been challenged. Either because he intimidated people enough to back down, or the people he ran with did. And he had the overconfidence to prove it.

Tate smiled and looked over at the man who still had a hold of Adam. "Now he has nothing to say. That's usually how it works with these so called tough guys when reality sets in."

"Oh," Walker finally broke. "You want reality?"

Taylor jumped up from her seat. "It's fine. Let's just leave. The police will be here in a minute. This isn't your fight."

Tate laughed. "She's got a good leash on you there. Seems like you should probably listen to her before you get hurt. That's what happens to people who don't mind their own business." Tate laughed again. Walker guessed that Tate thought what he was about to say was going to be funny. But Walker knew it was going to get Tate hurt. So he waited for the punchline.

Tate was eyeing Taylor now. "Speaking of leashes . . ."

Walker interrupted, "I'm going to give you one chance to not finish that sentence. I'll walk away if you don't."

Tate shared a laugh with the man holding Adam by the shirt. Then he brought his eyes straight to Walker's. Walker felt his fist clench.

"Speaking of leashes, that's a damn fine looking bitch you've got there."

"Walker, no!" Taylor shouted as she grabbed for his arm. But he was already gone.

As Walker stalked forward, Tate brought back his right hand. When he launched it forward, Walker looked down, showing Tate the top of his head. When Tate's fist smashed against the top of Walker's skull, everyone on that deck could hear the bones in Tate's hand snap. In a blink, Walker could see Tate for the man—or lack thereof—that he really was.

"Mr. Walker, don't!" Adam shouted. "These guys—"

Before Adam could finish, the man holding him shoved him to the ground. Walker knew he could turn his focus to the dark-haired, broad-shouldered man, because Tate was already finished. He was leaning against the deck's side rail, moaning as he stared at his lifeless hand. The dark-haired man reached inside the lapel of his black sport coat, so Walker closed the distance.

Before the man could pull what Walker had to assume was a firearm, he push-kicked forward, turning the man's left knee awkwardly. With the man's focus on what was inside his jacket, and now his knee, it was easy for Walker to follow up with a vicious left hook to the man's jaw. As blood splattered toward the onlookers, Walker reached out and caught the man's arm that was inside his jacket, and took the pistol from his hand as he fell unconscious. Before the second spare man at the table could pull his gun, Walker had already turned the one he'd just taken toward him and held it to his neck.

The bouncer had regained consciousness, ran over, and pulled the arms of the man under Walker's gun back behind his back.

"Adam, can you make sure the unconscious one doesn't have any other weapons?"

Adam responded by moving quickly to the floor of the deck and searching the man.

"Who the hell are you?" Tate said. His voice trembled. He was clearly in a lot of pain.

Walker ignored him and looked back at Taylor. She nodded her head sideways, clueing Walker that it was time to go. Walker turned back to Tate.

"Some advice?"

"Eat shit," Tate said. "You already know you're going to pay for this."

"Never challenge a man you don't know to a fight. Especially when you have to rely on your friends to actually do the fighting."

"I'll find out who you are," Tate said.

Walker moved his head over to the women Tate was with. "Some advice for you then?"

Walker was in a giving mood.

The two ladies looked over at Tate, then back to Walker. They weren't sure what to say.

Walker finished his thought. "The only thing you'll ever get from a loser, is losing. You can do better."

Walker's *scintillating* advice was punctuated by the whoop of a siren arriving. He walked over to Taylor and took her by the hand.

"The police are going to want to talk to you," a man in a Caddy's polo said.

Walker imagined he was the manager. "No comment."

"Dad advice?" Taylor smiled as they walked away. "Really?"

"I'll find you, you son of a bitch!" Tate shouted at Walker's back.

Walker ignored it as he and Taylor walked past people who'd been too intrigued to stop watching the train-wreck that had just happened. He smiled at Taylor. "Dad advice or not, it was good advice."

Taylor laughed. "Can't argue with that."

CHAPTER SIX

Taylor had driven to Caddy's that evening, but she decided to leave her car parked. One, she had a few drinks in her system, and a DUI really doesn't look good on an FBI agent's resume. But two—and Walker's favorite reason—she had decided to have a night cap with Walker, and it was as good of a night as any to take the short stroll back over the bridge to the Yacht & Tennis Club.

"Have you always been a bar fight kind of guy?" Taylor said as she walked beside him as they both stepped onto the bridge's pedestrian walkway.

Walker smiled. The lights were making Taylor's hair glow in the night. "First one, actually."

"Really? None in college, or the military?"

"Never been to college, or the military. And you don't have to mask your questions. You can just ask. I'll choose if I want to answer or not."

Taylor laughed. "Okay. Fair enough."

"What?"

"You're just . . . different." Taylor quickly reached over and grabbed his hand. "I don't mean that in a bad way."

"Is there any other way?"

"Different can be very good, if it's the right kind."

"Mine the right kind?"

She looked over at him as a car passed on the road. Her smile was glowing now. "I think so."

"You think so?" Walker said. "Not exactly a glowing review."

"Don't take it like that. I'm just getting to know you. You just . . . have a very matter of fact way about you, that is totally great. It's just not what I'm used to."

"Let me guess—"

Taylor interrupted."Oh no, more self-analyzation?"

"It's the only trick I've got," Walker said.

"Fair enough."

Walker looked her up and down. "I'm guessing you're used to guys throwing on the charm. First they compliment your looks, then maybe your accent. Definitely how nice you look in that dress. Maybe even go so far as to tell you that you have a great body. Am I close?"

"Well . . . you're not wrong."

"And they, of course, would never say anything that could ever be construed as a negative. Even if it were clearly true. Because they wouldn't want to offend you, thus ruining their chances with such a beautiful woman."

Taylor laughed and ran her fingers through her hair. "Like I said, Walker, you are the smoothest, un-smooth guy I've ever met. You just found a way to compliment me, without making it seem like it was coming from you. Didn't you?"

"Honestly? Not intentionally. But all of it is true."

"And it is true that it is what I'm used to. So, even though it's different that you aren't afraid to say what you feel, it's a good thing. Makes you easier to trust. But . . . that's probably your plan."

"Right or wrong, I'm me," Walker said.

Several cars passed them in a row when the light behind them turned green. They'd made it to the end of the bridge and Walker punched the crosswalk button.

"So back there, if not military, then what? Because clearly you've been thoroughly trained."

"Lets call it military-adjacent?" Walker said.

"Vague, but I'll let it pass."

They crossed the street and just as they were about to turn left off the sidewalk to go through the gate at the condo complex, two police cars went by. They both noticed.

"There's a reason I didn't want you to get involved back there, even though I know you really didn't have a choice."

"They were some bad men. I get it."

"Yes," Taylor said as she let Walker lead her through the gate, then on through the dark parking lot. "But it's more than that. A lot of the crime and drugs has been moving North from Miami lately. All the cartels and such have the big cities either thoroughly divided at this point, or fully covered with their own system. They've learned that fighting over territory is much less profitable than moving into the smaller surrounding areas. Plenty of untapped users, without all the violence to procure them."

"Why'd they wait so long?"

"Not sure, but it's moving fast now. Everyone has caught on."

Walker opened the first door to his condo complex, tapped in the door code, then held the door open for Taylor.

"So now the violence is coming to the smaller cities?" Walker said. "The cartels starting to fight over those?"

"Yes, but right now it's more about establishing the territory. So the cartels are sending their most violent men from places like Miami to make sure no one gets in the way of the new trade in places like Tampa, and unfortunately, even places like here in St. Pete."

Walker tapped the elevator button. The lobby was cool. He could see that it had given Taylor a chill as she rubbed her arms. "And you think maybe I just roughed up some of those violent men?"

The elevator dinged and they stepped on. Walker pressed the nine.

"Not sure," Taylor said. "That was just my concern. But you handled it well."

"If that's their most violent, it shouldn't be hard to run them out."

"Yeah, well . . . it's when they all have their guns that it seems to be more of a problem."

Walker smiled as the elevator door opened. He placed his hand at the small of Taylor's back and once they stepped out, he guided her left along the walkway. The sun was gone, but just passed the lights of the buildings in the distance the black void of the ocean was easy to see.

"What about you?" Walker said. "How long have you been an agent?"

They came to the last door and Walker stepped in front of Taylor to unlock it. He opened it as she answered.

"Long enough to see a major shift in the bay area. And not a good one."

Walker followed Taylor inside. She walked passed the kitchen and through the living room directly to the sliding glass door. "Nice place. You mind? I'm a little chilly."

"Of course not."

Walker moved toward her and followed her out onto the balcony. He slid the door shut behind him. The breeze was warm. The lights of the houses lining the intracoastal showed where the waterway extended out in front of them. Taylor breathed in the sea air, then turned toward Walker, leaning back against the rail. The yellow light from inside gave Walker a better view than could ever exist beyond that rail.

"Well . . . sorry if I inadvertently caused you any trouble tonight," Walker said.

"You mean by helping a defenseless bartender and a damsel waitress in distress? You hardly had a choice." She smiled. As she did, he felt as though she looked right through him. "Besides, pretty sexy to see a man stand up for someone."

"Yeah?" he said.

"Yeah."

Taylor's eyes danced between his, and his lips. He could feel what she wanted. Walker wanted the same. He stepped forward and wrapped his arm around her waist as she brought her hands to his face. She pulled him down to her as he pulled her in. Her lips were sweet with wine. He could feel her heart thudding against him as they pressed together. Her breath was hot as she moved down his neck. The hairs on his arms stood on end.

He reached back and slid the door open. Then lifted her and she wrapped her legs around his waist.

"No night cap then?" Walker said, smiling.

Taylor pulled her lips from him and leaned back. There was a wild in her eyes. She plunged back in, taking his lips in hers. She finished by nibbling at his bottom lip. Then she whispered, "I'll be your night cap."

Not another word was spoken for a very long time.

CHAPTER SEVEN

Walker toweled off as he stepped out of the shower. He'd done his best to lay in bed until Taylor woke up. Well, maybe it wasn't really his best. He'd only laid there for about five minutes. That was an hour and a half ago at 5:00 am. He felt as though his body might catch on fire if he'd laid there a second longer. So he did what any completely abnormal man with at beautiful, naked woman lying in bed beside him would do . . . he'd gotten up and went for a five mile run.

The sun still wasn't up, and neither was Taylor. He tossed his towel over the shower curtain rod, turned off the bathroom light, and carefully opened the bathroom door. Doing his very best not to wake her. He pulled back the sheet and slinked into bed. He let out a sigh. Job well done.

"Eventful morning Mr. Walker?" Taylor said softly.

Maybe not so well done.

"Sorry, didn't mean to wake you. I'm an early riser."

It was still dark outside, which meant it was still pitch black in the room. But he heard her side of the bed shuffle in the sheets.

"No," she said, now facing him, "I'm an early riser. You just don't sleep."

There was a sweet mint smell coming from Taylor. Not the morning breath he'd expected.

"How'd you brush your teeth while I was in the shower?"

"I don't have a toothbrush here, silly. I wasn't expecting to go home with you so I wasn't prepared."

"Yet your breath is minty fresh."

"It's gum," Taylor said.

"Is that like your morning coffee?"

Taylor laughed. "It's my morning breath killer. That way when I'm on top of you, it won't turn you off."

Walker felt her hand move to a place that he very much welcomed.

The two of them made love again.

Somewhere near a half an hour of fun later, Taylor rolled over from on top of Walker and the two of them lay in their own sweat, panting.

"So much for that shower," Taylor said, breathless.

Walker laughed. "Worth it."

"Totally worth it."

Taylor's phone began vibrating on the nightstand beside her. "Perfect timing. My turn for a shower. You mind?"

"Not at all. Clean towels in the closet."

Walker felt Taylor roll onto him. Then he felt her lips softly on his. "This was nice," she said after pulling away.

Walker wrapped his arms around her and pulled her in for one more kiss. "It really was."

Taylor rolled away and answered her phone. "Agent Crenshaw." A pause. "It's awfully early don't you think?"

Walker listened to her voice trail off into the bathroom. He reached over and flipped on the lamp just in time to see the back of her beautiful body disappear into the bathroom.

He used his towel to clean up a bit, then went to the closet and grabbed a black v-neck tee and a pair of grey joggers.

He gave Taylor her privacy and went to make coffee. As he read a bit of his novel, Niceville, by Carsten Stroud, he heard the shower cut off, and then the hair dryer. He definitely wasn't used to having sounds of another human in the same space he occupied. It was a pleasant mix of comfort, and anxiety. Sweet and sour so to speak. But when he saw Taylor walk out of the room, once again in her white dress, sour would be the furthest description he'd ever find to describe her.

"Do I smell coffee?"

Walker smiled, got out of his seat, and went to pour her a cup.

"You look gorgeous this morning," he told her.

She curtseyed, "Thank you." She walked up, took the filled mug, dropped off a kiss and a smile.

"Thank you." He brushed her blonde hair back behind her ear. "Crime fighting starting early this morning?"

She sighed as she stepped back and leaned against the counter. "It seems it's on a never-ending loop."

"Job security," he winked.

"You sound like my dad." She sipped her coffee. "What's on your docket for the day? Fishing? Sailing? What does a retired thirty-something do with all his free time?"

"Workout down in the gym. Laps in the pool. A little light reading by the water."

"Tough job," she said.

"Somebody's gotta do it."

"Will I see you again, or was this just some one time fun?"

Walker smiled. "It was twice, and I would very much like to see you again."

Taylor laughed. "Well, I have to run." She looked down at her dress. "This isn't exactly government approved attire."

"Yeah, I don't imagine the boys at the office would get a lot of work done with you prancing around in that. I'll walk you out."

"All the way to my car, at Caddy's? We decided to leave it there, remember?"

"I do," Walker said reaching beside her on the counter and picking up a set of keys. "I went for a run this morning. Thought it would be easier to have it here waiting for you."

"Cute, and chivalrous, eh?" She took the keys, then pulled him close. "Thank you."

They kissed. Walker then produced a to-go cup for her coffee.

"And brains?" she said.

"Total package."

Walker grabbed some socks, threw on his shoes, and escorted Taylor to her car. The sun was on the rise. Soon temperatures would be too. He opened the door to her white Lexus SUV and stood inside the open door as she sat behind the wheel.

"I'm a newbie here," he said, "but I heard this Italian place called Matteo's in downtown St. Pete is really good. You heard of it?"

Taylor started the car. "It's delicious." Then a wry smile. "Why ever do you ask?"

"If it's good I want to take you there. Preferably tonight."

Her face hardened a bit with a furrowed brow. "Let me see what things are looking like at the office. Apparently there's chatter of something going down. I don't want to tell you yes and then have to bail. But I do want to go."

"I get it. I could never find time to have a date when I was in the game."

Taylor raised an eyebrow. "*In the game*, he says. Yeah, I'm going to have to know a little more about that."

Walker threw up his hands. "Classified." Then did then old zip the lip and lock it.

"You realize I already know how to unlock those lips, right?" She reached up, mimicked unlocking them, then leaned in for a long kiss.

After a moment, Walker pulled back. "You'd better go. Otherwise I'm going to have to hold you hostage."

Taylor shoved him away playfully. Then she shut her door and rolled down the window as she put on her sunglasses. She looked like a model. "Somehow I don't think I'd be mad about it." She put the SUV in reverse. "I'll text you. Have a good day, okay handsome?"

"My day has already been made."

Taylor flashed him a smile, then drove away. His body ached for her as he watched her leave. Not a feeling he was used to. Also not one he was mad about. He turned, looked over at the sun, took a deep breath and didn't dare stifle the smile he was wearing. So far he really liked St. Pete. Maybe he would wait a little longer to find that trouble he thought he would look for.

If that trouble, of course, hadn't already found him.

CHAPTER EIGHT

Walker ran back upstairs to grab the novel he was reading and changed into his swimming trunks. He'd made a habit of reading by the water after hitting the weight room and swimming laps. He was already hungry after his run but he wasn't all that much of a breakfast guy so food could wait.

The gym at the Yacht & Tennis Club wasn't much bigger than a good sized living room. Free weights were close to the window. A couple of benches in front of them, and then a few treadmills, stairclimbers, and stationary bikes finished off the furnishings. There was a couple of televisions, one was on Fox News, the other ESPN. Walker wasn't interested in either one.

Walker waived to Carol when he walked in. She was a heavy set lady with a bushy brown hairdo. She was always on the bike, moving her legs at the speed of molasses. But at least she was moving.

"Good morning young man," she said. It's what she always said. It seemed to Walker that when people made it to a certain age they divided everything into young and old.

Maybe everyone did it. Even the young ones. For some reason it struck him as odd that day.

"Good morning, ma'am. You working up a sweat?"

"Eh, no more than I do when I walk to the refrigerator, but I tell myself that this is good for me."

"Well then, it's good for you, right?"

"That's right."

Walker moved past her and set his book down on the chair close to the free weights. There was one other person in the gym and he was doing shoulder presses. Walker noticed he was super fit, and though he had gray hair, he was younger than most of the snowbirds in the condo. Walker gave him a nod of hello when the man looked over. That's when he noticed his tattoo of a skull wearing a green beret.

"Thank you for your service," Walker said as the man set down his dumbbells.

The man grabbed a towel and wiped off. "It was my pleasure. You serve? You look like you've got the build."

"Not in an official capacity," Walker said. He should have just said no.

"Odd answer. But I know we have a large piece of our military that works very unofficially. So thank you for your service."

"No thanks needed," Walker said.

The man stepped forward with an outstretched hand. His white-stubbled, chiseled jaw matched the rest of his carved frame. The green in his eyes matched the green beret painted on his shoulder. Walker stepped forward and they exchanged a firm handshake.

"Jonathan James," the man said.

Walker did his best not to make a face. He couldn't believe he'd just heard Taylor mention this man's name last night as Tate James' father, and now he had run into him here at the condo exercise room.

"Tom Walker." He had all but quit using his alias of David it seemed. Something he wasn't happy with himself about, but it felt wrong lying to the man for some reason.

"Nice to meet you," Jon said. Then he pointed to the novel Walker set on the chair. "Big reader?"

"Big reader. Lot of downtime in what I used to do for a living."

"I hear that. What is it? It any good?"

"Niceville by Carsten Stroud. Third time reading it."

"Enough said," Jon said as he wiped his forehead with his towel. "I'll have to check it out. I'm reading Dead Fall by Brad Thor right now. The man does his research."

"Haven't read him but I've heard great things."

"Good stuff. You live in the building?"

Walker's lizard brain spoke to him. Was this Tate's father coming for revenge? Could this not be a coincidence at all? Walker was trying to check his skepticism, but for the moment it wasn't easy.

"Temporarily," Walker said. "Call it a staycation I guess. Still trying to figure out how to be retired."

"Awfully young to be retired. Must have done well for yourself."

"How long have you had a place here?" Walker said, bypassing Jon's comment.

"Me? I don't live here. I'm in a house just across the inlet over there." Jon pointed passed the pool that was just outside the gym's window. "I have a couple of properties I'm renovating here though, so they let me use the gym. Good money in that if you're retired, and not a lot of work. Happy to share some contacts with you if you're interested."

Share contacts? Not the sort of thing a man would do if he wanted revenge for breaking his son's hand.

"I always did like real estate. I appreciate that."

"I'll let you get to your workout," Jon said. "It was nice to meet you."

Jon started to back away for the gym door.

"You too. I'll give Brad Thor a try."

"You won't be disappointed." Jon turned to walk away, then he stopped an turned back to Walker. "Listen, you a gun guy?"

Was this where it went sideways?

Walker nodded. "Other than books, it's really the only thing I do."

Jon smiled. "Yeah, I figured. Listen, I've got some special guns, and not a lot of friends in St. Pete. I actually live most of the time in Miami. But if you want, I'm going to hit the range around lunch. We could grab a bite then put some holes in some shit."

Walker wasn't much of a "spend time with strangers" type of guy. Especially when said stranger was a criminal arms dealer who might be into even more nefarious things with his son. But there was something about Jon that he really liked. And he didn't seem to know Walker at all. That's the read Walker was getting anyway. Besides, he might be able to help Taylor out some if he got a little insider information on Jon James. So, he decided to play along.

"Okay," Walker said. "Sounds great actually."

"All right. Meet you out front here close to the gate . . . say, 11:30?"

"Works for me. See you then, Jon."

"See you then."

Jon nodded to Carol on his way out the door. The last few days were full of surprises for Walker. This one, however, had to be near the top. He hoped Jon wasn't there looking to meet the man who'd hurt his son, because he seemed like a decent guy. And, right or wrong, the fact that he'd served in the military gave him a longer leash in Walker's eyes.

Walker wasn't sure what vibe he was putting out to attract new people into his life, but he sure hoped to continue the streak. For the first time in his entire life he was bringing decent people around. A stark contrast to the monsters he'd been socializing with his, well, his entire life. Or, with Jon, it could be more of the same. But he was going to at least stick around and find out.

"Sounds like a fun day for you boys," Carol said as she sloth'd her way off the exercise bike. "He's in here a lot lately. Always been really kind."

That an informational step in the right direction. At least there was some corroboration that Jon wasn't only there to see if he could find Walker.

"Thanks Carol," Walker said, then smiled. "You want to go to the gun range? I've got a real smooth shooting AR-15 you would look good handling."

Carol laughed as she toweled away the phantom sweat from her brow. "Yeah? Only thing I shoot these days are pills young man. But you two enjoy. I'll see ya tomorrow morning."

"Have a good one."

"You too, handsome."

Walker noticed himself smiling in the mirror as she walked away. It was a very peculiar look to find on his face. Happy. Something he wasn't sure he'd ever been as long as he'd been living. Now he just hoped it wasn't a short-lived feeling.

CHAPTER NINE

Jon's burner phone began ringing as he pulled away from the Yacht & Tennis Club. He didn't recognize the number so there was only one person it could be.

"Bud Scarberry," Jon answered the phone.

"How the hell are you old pal?" Bud said. His voice deep and gruff as if he'd smoked two packs a day for the last thirty years.

"Better now, hopefully."

"Right to it then, huh? Sounds like trouble. How bad is it?"

Jon pulled into his driveway and put his car in park. "The kind I hate getting you involved in, but really have no other choice."

"That bad, huh?"

"That bad." Jon shut his car door and started his way toward the back of the house. He was feeling anxious. The water always helped calm him. "Where the hell are you in the world? You're like ricochet rabbit. I can never keep track of you."

"I know. I usually am. But I'm in Tampa right now. Just got off a job."

"Tampa? Hell, you're close. I'm here in St. Pete Beach."

"No shit?" Bud said. "I've got some loose ends to tie up this evening, but I could come down tomorrow if you need me too."

"Well, I want you to no matter what. It's been too long. But I want to tell you what the hell is going on before you come down to get involved in anything. I'm hoping you'll just be able to pass me off to a contact you might have. Not wanting to actually get you involved."

"Okay. Any contact in particular?"

Jon sighed. "This is where it gets tricky. You on a secure line?"

"Always when I call you," Bud said with a laugh. "You're always trying to get me in trouble."

"Yeah. Pot calling the kettle black there my friend."

"Maybe so. Just spill it. It can't be that bad."

Jon paused for a minute as he approached the edge of the property and looked out over the intracoastal. The water was calm. There wasn't a lot of traffic buzzing by. The exact opposite was going on in his mind.

"I need to get rid of 250 kilos of cocaine."

"250 kilos? Jon! Drugs? I never thought—"

"I know, Bud. I don't need a lecture. And I don't sell drugs. I—"

"It sure as hell does sound like you sell drugs to me, Jon. Holy hell. That's like, what, seven million dollars?"

"Seven and a half actually. But I don't sell drugs. You know me. But my son botched an arms deal to the wrong guy and there was a drug shipment that was being piggybacked on the deal that we didn't know about. Both were stolen."

"Jesus H. Tate's not that guy that can pull that off, Jon. You know that. What the hell are you doing?"

"It was a mistake. I put who I wanted Tate to be in front of who he is. Won't happen again."

"I'd say not. Did Tate survive it?"

Another pause. "For now."

"What kind of guy are we talking about here?" Bud said. "Who exactly did Tate shit on? Has to be a big fish."

"I'd rather not say, Bud. Really. Just know it's trouble I can't get out of. And I just need to know if you know anyone who can move that kind of weight."

"I'm not a drug dealer either, Jon. You—"

"I know you're not, but don't bullshit. You Merc for plenty of guys involved in the trade."

This time Bud paused. "I hear what you're asking me old friend. And maybe I can help. But my name could still be thrown around and I won't get involved in anything where I don't know all the players."

Jon understood. He would say the same thing. But Bud would be absolutely out of his mind to get involved with Javier Vasquez. Just like Jon lost his mind when he dealt with him.

"Jonny?"

"I hear you, Bud. And I get it. But you're not going to like it."

"Yeah, I suppose not. But out with it so we can move on."

"Javier Vasquez," Jon blurted.

"*What?*" Bud's baritone voice went up an octave. "Head of the Juarez Cartel—Javier Vasquez? Have you lost your fuckin' mind?"

"I know, Bud. I know."

"Do you?"

"It was supposed to be my last trade. Get one last big one done and move on to real estate investing."

"And you picked maybe the most dangerous man in the free world for your last hoorah?"

"I did. Can we move on now?"

Bud laughed. "Yeah, we can move on. As friends. But I can't get involved in this shit. This is way over our heads my friend."

"All I have to do is sell the 250 kilos and give Vasquez the money for it. That's it. Then it's squashed."

"Buddy. I love ya, but Jon, you're smarter than that. A guy like Vasquez finds out you know how to move 250 kilos and he'll make sure you do it over and over again for him. Those guys are like vampires. Once they get their teeth in you, they turn you, and you're with them until the sunshine burns you into ash."

"Turns me into ash? You're being a little dramatic now, Bud."

"I'm not being nearly dramatic enough. This is some real deep shit here. A quicksand pond of shit."

"Yeah. It is. And I was hoping you'd be there to throw me a rope. Not step on my head."

"Jonny, your boy Tate already stepped on your head. And I'd need an excavator to get you out of this, not a damn rope."

"And that's exactly why I called you," Jon said as he kicked at the short concrete wall that separated his yard and the water. He absolutely despised the fact that he was tail tucked begging his friend. But he had also bailed Bud out of a couple bad situations of his own. Bud knew it too."

"Let me make a couple of calls."

"I knew I could count on you."

"If I can help get you clear of this, that makes us even. This is as much me saving your life as you saved mine back in Iraq."

"Bud, I couldn't agree more."

"Talk soon."

The call dropped. Jon closed his phone and put it in his

pocket. He didn't know if Bud would actually be able to help, but it felt good to have that conversation behind him. He was happy he'd met that Tom Walker fella at the gym. He didn't know what he would do if he had to hang around that empty house all day by himself. Going and shooting some guns would be as good as therapy. And God knows he needs that.

His phone began buzzing in his pocket again. This number was not a US number. A lump formed in his throat.

"Mr. Vasquez," Jon answered.

"Ah, if it isn't my favorite arms dealer who's about to get all my missing money back to me."

"I'm in St. Pete Beach, Florida. You'll need to drop the product here. A place called Sea Hags. It's right on the intracoastal. One in the morning works best for me. Can you get it ready by tomorrow night?"

"Straight to business. Quite different than your son. I like it. Of course I can have it ready. There a place for a boat at this, Sea Hags?"

"Small marina right in front of it. No one will be the wiser."

"They'd better not be."

Jon ended the call. Just the sound of Vasquez's voice made his skin crawl. He couldn't believe he'd let himself deal with such a snake. The only trick now was to avoid the venom.

CHAPTER TEN

WALKER SLID HIS SIG SAUER P365 EDC INTO HIS concealed hip holster and threw on his back pack full of spare rounds. Then he grabbed his Daniel Defense AR-15 in its black nylon tactical scabbard and threw it over his shoulder. It was just before 11:30. He locked up and headed for the elevator. The outside walk was muggy, but somewhat masked by the breeze that was blowing on the sixth floor. Down at pavement level it would be much steamier. He wasn't sure what he was walking into with Jon James, but he was going to give it the benefit of the doubt until Jon gave him a reason otherwise.

As he got into the elevator, an old man was admiring Walker's luggage, but his assumed wife seemed a bit more concerned. Her eyes were wide as she stared at the butt of his AR-15 as it extended out beyond its scabbard.

"Goin' to war are ya, son?" the old man said in that typical airy old man voice.

"Just going to get some practice in."

"Well let me know what condo you're stayin' in, that way if the shit hits the fan, we can come to you."

The woman turned around and slapped at the man. "Oh Harry. Leave the poor boy alone."

Walker smiled. "Ninth floor, all the way to the left."

"I used to be a good shot," the old man said. "World War 2."

"Then I'll definitely welcome you to my place if said shit does ever hit. You can protect me."

"I'd be proud to do it."

The elevator opened. Walker motioned for the couple to go first. "Thank you for your service, sir. And you ma'am for loaning him to us."

The man just nodded with a smile. "You have a good one, now."

"You too."

The woman whispered to her husband as they walked into the lobby, "Such a nice young man."

Walker smiled and moved in the opposite direction and out the front doors. There was an old school, royal blue Ford Bronco waiting at the curb.

"I see you brought some toys," Jon said out the window.

"Can't go to a party without any favors."

Walker moved around the front, opened the back passenger door and slid his rifle in, then got in the front seat.

"Mr. Walker," Jon said, holding out his fist.

Walker gave it a bump with his knuckles. "Mr. James."

Jon put the Bronco in drive and pulled forward. "I had something come up so I don't have as long as I'd hoped. Mind if we skip lunch? I can get you something from a drive through if you're hungry."

"Don't mind at all. I had a big breakfast."

"I hate changing things up, but it's one of those things I can't move."

"No worries at all."

Walker couldn't help but let his mind wander to what

exactly Jon might have to change things up for. Did his son call him? Was there a new client he needed to supply with guns?

"Thank you." Jon pointed across Walker's chest to his right. "Would you look at that beauty?"

Walker followed Jon's finger and found his own silver '67 Mustang GT500 fastback glistening in the sun.

"She drives better than she looks."

"No shit? That's yours?"

"Pride and joy."

"I bet," Jon said as he pulled away from the condo complex. "I knew I liked you. Young man with that kind of taste can't be bad."

"Wait till you see me shoot."

A few minutes later Jon pulled the Bronco into the back of what looked like a small abandoned warehouse.

Walker took a long look at the dilapidated metal building. Even if he wasn't worried about Jon setting him up for a little revenge he'd be a bit worried about pulling up to an abandoned building with a car full of weapons. "If I didn't know better, I'd think you were bringing me here to kill me."

Walker was kidding, but not kidding.

"Yeah, couldn't take you to an actual gun range. Some of the guns I like to shoot aren't exactly legal in the states."

"I knew I liked you," Walker said with a laugh as he played it off.

When Jon was getting out of truck an envelope fell out of his pocket onto the seat. Walker was reaching back to grab his rifle and happened to glance and see the address. It only stood out because it was 9555 Blind Pass Rd, somewhere on the same road Walker's condo complex sat. Maybe Jon had an office somewhere near the Yacht & Tennis Club. Walker got his rifle and exited the Bronco. Jon was standing outside with an oversized duffel bag that bulged at the sides. Walker followed him around the corner to a side door where Jon used a key to unlock it. They stepped inside, and when Jon flipped a couple of switches, some overhead florescent lights buzzed to life. The building was mostly empty save for the three gun range slots on the left side.

"It ain't much," Jon said, "but it gets the job done."

"Ever have neighbor complaints?"

"Buildings on both sides are empty for now. So no."

Walker followed Jon over to the target area. The rest of the building was mostly scraps, and a lot of old shelving from the previous tenant.

"All right, you've got me curious," Walker said. "What's in the bag?"

Jon bent over and unzipped. "Mostly standard stuff. Except for this refurbished beauty here . . ."

Jon pulled a rifle from the bag. Even without the bayonet at the end, Walker could tell by the worn black walnut stock that it was something vintage. Something Walker, a certified gun expert knew nothing about. His knowledge only consisted of modern weaponry.

"Definitely a beauty," Walker said.

Jon handed it over. The rifle was heavy, and solid as the tree it was cut from.

"What am I holding?"

Jon smiled. Walker could see the pride in his eyes. "So you like old cars, but not old guns?"

"Oh, I like them. Just have no experience with them."

"That there is an M1 Garand. World War Two. It took me a while, but I finally got her sited in."

"Heavy."

"Yep," Jon said. "Even without the bayonet. Nine and a half pounds."

Jon bent down and reached in the bag again. He pulled

out an eight round enbloc clip and loaded it into the M1. "Now just push the operating rod."

Walker did as he asked.

"She's ready to fire. .30-06 rounds. Let's see what you've got?"

Walker stepped forward and grabbed the noise canceling earmuffs that were hanging from a screw and put them on. He looked back at Jon to make sure he had done the same. About a hundred feet down range there were hanging metal plates. Walker pulled the rifle up to his shoulder and stared down the sites. He couldn't imagine lugging one of those guns around in battle. His DD AR-15 only weighed six and a half pounds. That extra three pounds would get awfully tiresome if one was doing a lot of shooting.

Walker took a deep breath as he took aim at the center plate. He gently squeezed the trigger and even through his ear protection the rifle boomed inside the building. And seemingly just as loud was the plink made when he hit the target.

"Nice one!" Jon's muffled voice came through. "Solid, right?"

Walker held up a thumb.

"All right now, show off a little!"

Walker moved the rifle left and fired twice. Then back to the middle for two shots. Then he finished off the target on the right, hitting it all three times.

"Whoo! Nice!" Jon shouted.

Walker made sure the chamber was clear then lowered the weapon. He turned as he removed his ear protection. Jon was wearing a wide smile. Walker could feel that he was wearing one too.

"Just feels different, don't it?"

Walker reached up and gave Jon the high-five his hand was requesting. "It really does."

"Well, you would have made the old guys proud. You're a good shot. That's easy to see. No hesitation." Jon took the gun from Walker. "My turn now. See if I can keep up."

This was the moment where it would turn if it was going to. Jon would have a loaded weapon in his hand. Walker just hoped he wasn't the target. Turned out he wasn't as Jon began firing.

Jon kept up quite well with Walker's accurate shooting. He didn't miss a target either. For the next hour, the two of them ran through their weapons, each impressive in form. They had a good time slapping high fives and cracking jokes. Something Walker hadn't had a lot of experience with in his life, but he could definitely see the appeal after having lived it. Other than Tim Lawson, Walker had never really had another male friend. His life in the shadows made any relationships difficult. It was a nice change having someone to shoot guns, and shoot the shit with. And Walker found no reason to believe that Jon wasn't a nice guy who was just trying to be friendly. Maybe Taylor was barking up the wrong tree with the dad. Maybe it really was Tate who was the trouble maker. Dealing arms illegally obviously wasn't a legit way to make money, but it was—at least to Walker—a lot different than being a drug dealer. Though he couldn't for the life of him understand why.

The two of them packed up their things.

"I've got to run, Walker, but this has been fun. We should do it again if you're going to be in town a little longer."

"I will be. And I'd love to."

Walker followed Jon to the exit. Jon flicked off the lights as he pushed open the door. What was outside waiting for them wiped the smiles right off both of their faces.

CHAPTER ELEVEN

Walker took a step back when Jon stopped abruptly in front of him. Two new vehicles were parked beside Jon's blue Ford Bronco in the parking lot of the shooting range. A black SUV on the left, and a white sedan on its right. Both had three men standing at their rear. One of the men was leaning back against the trunk of the white car. Walker recognized him immediately. He was the same dark-haired man Walker had knocked out on the patio at Caddy's the night before. This time, he was holding a gun. More importantly, it didn't seem like these men knew Jon. Maybe he wasn't involved with his son Tate's affairs at all.

"Looks like a nice shiner you've got there," Walker said. "Let me guess, I should see the other guy?"

Jon turned to Walker. "You know these guys?"

Walker smirked. "I'm the 'other guy'."

The dark-haired man stood up from his leaning position. He didn't look happy.

"What?" Walker said. "Did I steal your speech about how I don't look so tough now that you're holding a gun?"

The guy beside the dark-haired man laughed. He took a pistol to the forehead for enjoying Walker's joke.

Jon looked back again. "Think you could maybe, I don't know, tone it down a little?"

Jon didn't look scared, but Walker knew he was poking the bear. He had his reasons. He obviously didn't want to get shot, but what he did want was to play to this gunman's sense of bravado. All of his boys were around him watching. Walker hoped he could goad him into a fist fight instead of him using his gun before Walker could get to his own.

"You think this is funny?" the dark-haired man said. He had a slight Hispanic accent.

"No," Walker said. "It just doesn't surprise me. I figured I might see you again after last night. And after I heard the type of people you associate with. I also figured you wouldn't be man enough to be unarmed. Guess I'm pretty good at figuring."

The dark-haired man smiled. "You have a bag of weapons there. What did you expect me to do?"

Walker pulled the strap of his AR-15 scabbard from around his neck and dropped it on the ground. Then he undid his concealed hip holster and tossed it on top of that.

Jon looked back at him like he was crazy.

"There," Walker said. "That better?"

Dark-haired man motioned toward Jon and his sack of toys.

Jon looked back again. "I hope you know what you're doing." Then he dropped his bag.

Jon definitely did not know these men his son was associating with.

"Step over here away from the weapons," Dark-haired Man motioned with his pistol to Walker's left.

Walker and Jon both took a few steps to their left. Walker keeping Jon just in front of him on his right.

"Your other friend still getting his hand taken care of?" Walker said. "Thought for sure I'd see the two of you together. Hard to fight a man with one hand though I guess."

"You have an awfully smart mouth for an unarmed man with a gun held on him."

Jon said, "Yeah, you sure do."

Walker nodded toward Jon. "He's not part of this. How about you let him go."

"That's not how this works," Dark-Haired Man said.

"I thought you might say that."

Walker shot his hand toward the belt-line of the back of Jon's jeans. Jon's EDC pistol was a Glock 17. No safety. So he knew he would have time to grab it and get a shot off before Dark-Haired Man even realized what was happening. When Walker squeezed the trigger as he raised the gun, Dark-Haired Man's hand exploded, and his gun fell to the asphalt. The man beside him went to reach down for it but Walker trained Jon's pistol on him.

"Don't do that," Walker said.

Jon reached down beside Walker and picked up Walker's pistol. A couple of the other men pulled their weapons. Dark-Haired Man was holding his arm, stifling cries of pain as blood dripped onto the ground. Walker had already made the assessment that these men, whatever gang affiliation they might have, were just a small-time outfit. Not the killers that Taylor had worried they might have pissed off. He knew it the second they didn't immediately shoot when he and Jon walked out the door. Real killers don't flinch. And they certainly don't have a conversation with the person with whom they are seeking their revenge.

"I could have killed you, but I didn't," Walker said.

Dark-haired Man looked up at Walker, fury in his eyes. "You think that's going to get you some sort of pass?"

Walker shrugged. "I could still kill you. Probably should I guess, seeing as how you clearly hold grudges."

"You can't kill all of us. You shoot me, there's no way you make it out of this parking lot alive."

Walker nodded as he looked at the other men who had stepped closer to him and Jon. "Okay. That's probably true. But . . . you'll still be dead."

Walker could tell that the man was thinking it over, even through the grimaces of pain. Walker had made a compelling argument by accurately shooting him in the hand without a lot of effort.

"Unsolicited advice?" Walker said. "Get to a hospital and get your hand looked at. And tell your friend Tate that this should be the last I hear from any of you."

Jon shot Walker a look. Walker didn't look away from Dark-haired Man.

"I know where you live," Dark-haired Man said.

"You sure you want to go down that road?" Walker said. "Right now I don't know your name. I don't know where you live. And I don't give a damn what you do for a living. Are you positive you want me to give a damn what you do for a living? Could be bad for business."

Walker knew that the man was caught between not wanting to look bad in front of his men, and making what everyone knew was a good decision.

"You a cop?" Dark-haired Man said.

"You a criminal?"

Dark-haired Man winced in pain again. Then he gave a knowing nod. He didn't say anything as he turned and nodded for everyone to leave. Probably best. At least he was smart enough to know that taking a loss is sometimes a win. All the men got back into their vehicles and drove away.

"You're still holding my gun," Jon said.

Walker held it down by his side and turned toward Jon. "Do I need it?"

"So you do know who I am."

"Only because of my encounter with your son last night. Who, by the way, doesn't seem much like you at all."

Jon nodded, then he turned Walker's pistol in his hand and held the butt end toward Walker. Walker did the same and they made the trade.

"That's because he isn't like me at all. What dumbshit thing did he do this time?"

"Sorry I didn't tell you when we first met," Walker said. "But I wasn't sure running into you in the exercise room was a coincidence, so I had to wait until I did."

"I would have done the same," Jon said. "How the hell did you cross paths with Tate?"

"I was having dinner at Caddy's when he and bullet-hand showed up with a few others. Let's just say they were rude enough to the staff that I had to get involved. And I tried really hard not to get involved."

Jon sighed and put his hand on his hip. "I don't know where the spoiled brat gets it. I don't know if it was his mother dying, or what, but that sounds like something he'd do. Unfortunately."

"Condolences on your wife."

"Thank you. It was a long time ago. So, you broke Tate's hand?"

"Technically he broke it on the top of my head. He's not much of a fighter."

"Fighter?" Jon said with a laugh. "The boy's a pussy, Walker. The worst kind. The kind who acts tough and can never back it up."

Walker nodded. He'd met many men like that along the way. "I have to ask," Walker said as he reattached his hip holster and put away his pistol. "You associated with what he's doing here in any way?"

"I actually told him he was completely cut off just yesterday if you can believe it. Whatever stupid shit he's into here, doesn't have my mark on it."

Walker believed him. It wasn't because he liked Jon, it was because when Jon talked about Tate, he could actually see the pain and anguish in the man's eyes.

"It's none of my business," Walker said, "I just like you. And was hoping these mutts we just turned away didn't have any affiliation to you."

"Sure didn't look like they do, did it?"

"No. I just had to ask."

"Pretty good trick pulling my gun and getting him shot before he could do anything."

"If that guy has ever shot anyone, I can assure you, it was an accident."

Jon laughed. "Well, either way, it was impressive. And definitely shows you're not just a range guy."

"No. Unfortunately, I've had far too much real world gun experience."

"Today it was fortunately. I haven't shot at anyone since the Army."

"That's a good thing." Walker picked up his AR. Jon grabbed his bag of weapons. "Jon, it isn't my place, but if you talk to Tate, maybe let him know I'm not really the right place to go looking for a fight?"

"Oh, I'm not going to just talk to him. I'm going whoop his ass like his mother should have when he was a kid. He definitely won't be a problem for you moving forward."

"Hope he's not for you either," Walker said as they moved toward Jon's Bronco.

Jon put his bag in the back, then let out another sigh. "I'm afraid a problem is all he'll ever be for me."

CHAPTER TWELVE

WALKER HAD JUST SET HIS THINGS DOWN IN THE CONDO when his phone started ringing. He couldn't help but smile when he saw that it was Taylor calling.

"I'm extremely busy at the moment," he answered. "I hope this is important."

Taylor laughed. "Yes, I'm sure the retired life has you exhausted with appointments and meetings."

"I'm a popular guy I guess."

Taylor's tone changed. "I know it's short notice, but I just pulled into the your parking lot. Do you have a few minutes?"

"You probably took everything I have this morning, but I can try again."

Taylor sighed. "Mmm. I wish this was a social call."

"Everything okay?"

"For now, yes. I just always like to stay ahead of things when the wind starts to blow a certain way."

"I'll be right down."

"Thanks."

Walker moved back outside, then caught the elevator

down. When the door opened, Taylor was standing there waiting. A smile on her face.

"Someone let me in."

Walker held out his hand to hold the elevator door. "Guess I'm going to have to reinforce the security around here."

She walked onto the elevator. "I just have one of those trustworthy faces, I guess."

He let go of the door and pushed the nine button. "I do like your face."

The elevator door closed. Taylor leaned into him for a long kiss. Walker didn't mind. She tasted like mint and smelled of wildflowers. Neither of them wanted to let go. The door opened to the ninth floor and an elderly couple stood waiting. Big smiles on both of their faces.

Walker pulled back when he noticed. "Sorry, let us get out of your way."

"Don't be sorry young man," the lady said. "Enjoy every second of her."

The old man gave him a wink and Walker took Taylor's hand to walk past them.

"Oh, he will," Taylor said.

Walker felt like a teenage kid getting caught by his parents.

"Have a good day," Walker said.

"I know you will," the lady said. "George and I already had our fun."

They walked into the elevator and Taylor leaned into him laughing. "I wanna be like them when I grow up."

"Not a bad goal to have," he said.

He let her inside and as soon as the door shut behind them, Taylor began undressing.

"I thought this wasn't a social call?" Walker said.

"It isn't. But I want you."

Twenty minutes later and Taylor rolled off of him gasping for air. They were both a mess of glistening sweat and passionate breaths—their bodies thrumming with pleasure.

"Wow," she said, panting.

Walker didn't speak. He just nodded as he let his eyes linger on her curves. He took in a deep breath through his nose and let it out through his mouth. "So . . . what was it you wanted to talk to me about?"

She rolled over, took him in with her eyes and laughed. "You're going to have to get dressed. I can't have a serious conversation with your muscles staring at me."

Walker grabbed his clothes and gave Taylor the room. When she walked out into the living room he had a bottle of water waiting for her.

"Thank you," she said. "Hard to be serious after that."

Walker motioned for the couch. "Lets get it over with then, so we can get back to not being serious."

They both had a seat and faced each other. Taylor's neck area was still a bit flushed beneath her white blouse.

"It's two things really," she said. "First, when I got to the office I did a little digging on Tate James and some of the people he's been associating with. It seems as though they are a small group of drug dealers around the Tampa area. They've had a few small-time run-ins. Mostly just possession and sales of narcotics. But a couple were violent."

Walker smiled. "You worried about me?"

"Well . . . I just . . . yes, okay? What you did at Caddy's was noble, but I just want you to know that it may have put you in danger. And I just want you to know they really might come after you."

"Too late."

Taylor furrowed her brow. "Too late? What do you mean?"

"I mean they already came after me. Just a little bit ago."

"What? Today? Are you all right?"

Walker looked over at the open door to the bedroom. "You tell me."

"I'm serious, Walker. What happened?"

"Should I start from the beginning?"

"This doesn't sound good."

"It's interesting, that's for sure."

Taylor crossed her legs and sat back. "Do tell."

"Well, I just got back from a shooting range with Jon James."

Taylor's mouth slacked open. "Jon James? As in Tate James' father?

Walker nodded.

"How the hell did that happen? You knew him and didn't say?"

"I met him this morning in the gym here. Nice guy."

"You don't find that awfully coincidental?" Taylor said.

"I did. That's why I went shooting with him. To find out if it was a coincidence or not."

"And?"

"I'm confident in saying it was absolutely a coincidence."

Taylor folded her arms across her chest. "How could you possibly know that?"

"Because these friends of Tate James that you were talking about, they met us outside of the gun range, with guns of their own."

Taylor sat forward. "What? They came after you? How are you just now telling me this?"

Walker bypassed the question. "They held the gun on Jon, too. They had no idea Jon was Tate's dad."

Taylor shook her head in disbelief. "So, they just let you go? I don't see a mark on you."

"They did just let us go. You could say that I sort of

forced their hand." It was a joke to himself. He actually laughed a little out loud.

"And you find this funny? That you had guns pulled on you."

"Now it's funny, yes."

"What does, *you forced their hand,* mean, exactly?" Taylor said, remaining unamused.

"I shot him. The dark-haired one from last night. Right in the hand. That's why it's funny."

Taylor gave him a blank stare.

"Forced their hand . . ."

"Oh, cause you shot him in the hand. Wow. A real comedian you are."

"Hey . . ."

"Sorry, Walker, but they could have killed you."

Walker shook his head. "No. No they couldn't have, actually."

Now Taylor shook her head. "So, now what? They come back even harder?"

"No. We came to an understanding. I may have let them believe that maybe I was law enforcement. And that maybe I would decide to not dig in on them if they just left it alone. They agreed and left."

"They said that? That they would leave it alone?"

"No, but it didn't have to be said."

"This is crazy, Walker. And what about Jon? What did he think was happening?"

"The dark-haired guy brought up Tate. After they left, Jon and I had a conversation about Tate. Turns out Tate is douchy enough that his own father doesn't like him."

"So he knows you broke Tate's hand?"

"He does."

"He's okay with that?"

"He was when I told him what happened. And he said

he'd make sure Tate didn't bother me again. Said he was going to kick his ass."

All Taylor could do was shake her head again. "This is all so strange."

"It is. But it's okay. And, Jon's actually a nice guy. I find it hard to believe that if you are looking into him for being into anything more than selling weapons that you would find anything."

Taylor gave him a faltering smile. "I like you, Walker. A lot, actually. But maybe, whatever you did before you retired . . . maybe judging people on the surface wasn't your strong suit?"

"I like you too, Taylor. Thank you. And maybe you're right. Most the men I went after I didn't have to pass judgement, because that was already done for me. It's why I was sent after them. But I'm telling you, Jon is a good guy."

"Yeah? Then why is he having an acquaintance of his lining up a large drug buy?"

Walker was quiet for a moment. He could see a large ferry boat passing through the intracoastal in the distance out the window to the balcony.

"Drugs?" Walker shook his head. "Listen, I'm not telling you that your intel is wrong. I'm not that arrogant."

"Thank you."

"But . . . If Jon really is mixed up in some sort of drug thing, I'm telling you, I just believe there is more to it for him. He's just not a drug guy. You've been doing this long enough, Taylor. You understand what I mean when I say that, right?"

Taylor nodded. "I do. I know what you mean. And maybe you're right. But the fact still remains that an old friend of his tried to line something up for Jon through one of our informants. And it's not a small amount of drugs."

"They mentioned Jon by name?"

"I really shouldn't be telling you any of this," Taylor said.

"Yet you have."

"Yes. His contact information was passed along."

Walker raised an eyebrow. "It's not like I haven't been wrong before. So, what are you going to do?"

Taylor smiled and scooted close. She ran her hand along his jawline.

Walker laughed. "Not tell me. I get it."

She leaned in for a kiss. She got one.

"That was all I had," Taylor said. "Didn't know you would actually have more to tell than me. And I know it goes without saying, but Walker—"

"Don't say anything to Jon. I understand."

"Thank you. Now, I gotta run. Jon was supposed to make contact with our informant this afternoon. Maybe there is some sort of mix up and Jon won't be involved."

"It's not like he's my friend," Walker said. "I just liked the guy. We still on for our date at Matteo's tonight?"

"You're not sick of me yet?"

Walker grabbed Taylor and pulled her close. Gave her a long kiss on the lips. Then pulled back. "I really don't think I am."

He began unbuttoning her blouse. She laughed as she slapped his hand away and stood up. "Good. I'll see you tonight then." Walker tugged at the waist of her pants. She slapped his hand away again. "But right now I've got to go. Save up that energy for later."

Walker fell back against the couch with a painful sigh. Taylor blew him a kiss and hurried out the door.

CHAPTER THIRTEEN

Jon pulled his Ford Bronco to a stop just across the street from the house his son Tate was renting. He wasn't surprised to see that the grass desperately needed cut. He told his son to rent a condo so he wouldn't have to deal with the yard maintenance, but of course, he hadn't listened. Jon wasn't sure what he was going to do at the moment. His initial intent had been to do just what he told Walker he was going to do, and kick his son's ass. But did he really have it in him? All he really wanted to do was convince Tate to go back to Miami and just stop making trouble.

Jon's phone started ringing. It was Bud.

Jon answered. "Tell me something good."

"I've got something good."

"I knew you'd come through."

"Well, it's not a done deal yet," Bud said. His voice sounded extra cranky. "This guy is no joke, Jonny. You sure this is what you want? Things go sideways, they're really sideways."

"I hear you, Bud. But you don't get more sideways than owing the Juarez Cartel."

"Okay. Just had to say it."

"Who is it?" Jon said.

"Vincent Delgado."

"Never heard of him."

"He's new in town," Bud said. "But he's growing fast."

"How quick can we get it done?"

"That's the other thing. My word don't mean shit to this guy really. So he says he needs to do what he does with every new client."

"All right. Which is?"

"A small trade. Just to make sure everything is what it's intended to be. I told him you are into guns."

"Damn it, Bud. I don't want this guy really knowing what I do."

"You said you were in a bad spot, right?"

"Yeah, but—"

"But nothing. He wasn't going to take you on cold. Not that much product. It sounds too much like a setup. And he's not wrong. I heard through the grapevine that he needed more weapons so I floated it. It changed his mind. You're welcome."

Jon was quiet for a moment. What could he say, really? He was absolutely in a bad spot and his old friend was just trying to help.

"Okay. I hear you."

"It has to be tonight," Bud said.

"Shit, that's fast. But I need it done fast. I can make it work."

"Where at? It needs to be somewhere local. And he only wants it done via the water."

"Perfect. Sea Hags in St. Pete Beach. I took the lease on the abandoned restaurant. There's a small marina right behind it. Give Delgado this number and I can pass along the details."

"Got it," Bud said. "And Jon?"

"Yeah buddy?"

"Bring your A team. No screwups. This guy is new, but legit. He comes down hard on people who mess up from what I've heard."

"No more screwups from my end old man. I'm running the show until it's over now."

"I'll pass things along. He'll be in touch."

"Thanks Bud."

"You got it."

The call ended. Jon's spirits were lifted and he suddenly didn't want to ruin it by talking to his degenerate son. And now he had work to do. Most of his team was in Miami. This would leave him short of his normal crew. He was going to have to make it work without them, and on top of that they would have to work fast to make sure everything was secure for that night. He pulled out his phone and called the man who'd been his most trusted for the last six years. Mark Jansen. Jon often referred to Mark as his guardian angel. He was certainly going to need him to get through the next few transactions.

"I figured I'd be hearing from you soon," Mark answered the phone. "You find a way to get us out of Tate mess?"

The word *us* didn't get past Jon. That was why he loved Mark. He was a full team player, no matter what the situation. The Green Beret in him wouldn't let him live any other way. Once he was committed, he was committed till the end. That, and Jon paid a whole hell of a lot better than any one else would. That too breeds loyalty. Mark was worth every penny. Jon knew he should have listened to Mark when he was adamant about not letting Tate run the shipment to the Juarez Cartel. So much so that Mark nearly walked away from Jon after that. Jon was glad he didn't.

"I think so," Jon answered. "I know we don't have the full

team in town but we have a deal to do tonight at Sea Hags. Meet me over there as soon as you can shake loose."

"Tonight?" Mark said. "Like you said, we're short manpower, Jon. You sure we shouldn't wait?"

"I would if I could. I'll stand in as one of the team on site. We good?"

"I'll be at Sea Hags within the hour."

"See you there."

Jon ended the call. He took one last look at Tate's house, then pulled his truck back out into the road. As bad as it sounded, his son just wasn't worth it. He hated that it had gotten to that point, but as his wife would always say, it is what it is. Jon had much bigger and more immediate fish to fry. So he dialed Javier Vasquez, anxious to relay some good news.

"Señor James," Vasquez answered. "I'm assuming this call brings good news for me."

"It does. I have a buyer. I should have your money to you very soon."

"That is good news Señor, but I do not want to hear what you will have. I want to hear what you have. So if you have a deal lined up, I suggest you make sure it goes through. I am not a very patient man."

Jon shook his head in disbelief. He couldn't wait to be through with this pain in the ass. "You got it."

"Don't mess this up again. I do not give third chances."

The call ended. Jon tossed his burner phone onto the passenger seat. He could see the light at the end of the tunnel. Now he just had to go and make sure he met that light with a done deal. Nothing else mattered at the moment.

CHAPTER FOURTEEN

Walker finished his second shower of the day as he wrapped his towel around his waist. The warm water reminded him of how long the day had already been. A run and a workout in the gym, two rounds in the bed with Taylor, target practice with some heavy weaponry, and of course, the standoff between he and Jon and the local drug dealers association.

For the last couple of hours he'd managed some time on the couch with a book. He wasn't a napper, but he felt himself dozing a few times. He was tired. But he had a beautiful woman awaiting his company, and the adrenaline from that alone would be enough to get him through.

Walker took the blow dryer to his hair. Before he put on the only semi-decently nice set of clothing he owned, he decided to reach for the cologne again. He could hear Tim Lawson laughing already at the story. But hey, the cologne worked the first time, why tempt fate?

As Walker pulled his black polo shirt over his head, he could hear his phone vibrating on the nightstand out in the bedroom. He walked over. It was Taylor.

Walker answered. "Just getting ready to leave. You sure I can't swing by and get you?"

"Hey," Taylor said. Walker could hear disappointment in her voice. "Don't hate me . . ."

"Pretty sure that's impossible. Something come up?"

"You know how I told you Jon James was mixed up in a drug deal?"

"Sure," Walker said.

"He linked up with our informant. They're doing a deal tonight."

"Really? So it really is drugs?"

"Well, it's not drugs tonight. This is just an initial small buy to make sure they are a good fit."

"You have to be there then. I totally get it."

"It's not till early in the am tomorrow, but we have to prepare. I'm really sorry."

"No, there's no need. I understand. I hate to hear that he's mixed up in that sort of thing. But I barely know the guy so it is what it is."

"I was really looking forward to dinner, and . . . after with you," she said.

"I know. Me too. But this is important. Promise me you'll be careful."

"Mr. Walker," Taylor laughed. "Do I detect that you care about my well being?"

"Of course. I don't have anyone else to sleep with so don't take that away from me," Walker joked.

"You're bad. But your jokes just might be growing on me."

"I'll take it," Walker said. "Listen, I really do understand. Be safe out there. I'll be here tomorrow."

"Thanks for getting it. And speaking of, I'll *get* out of you what you actually used to do for a living sometime soon. I can be very persuasive."

"Of that, I have no doubt. I look forward to your efforts."

"Talk to you soon."

"Bye Taylor."

Walker set his phone on the nightstand, then took a seat on the bed. He couldn't help but be disappointed. Disappointed in not being able to have dinner with Taylor, and what he'd learned about Jon. He didn't really know why he cared what Jon did, he just didn't seem like the type for drugs, and he'd thought Jon to be a genuinely nice guy. However, Walker knew he had about as little experience as any man in his thirties could ever have at judging what a good person or friend would be. He chalked his poor initial read up to inexperience, and more than likely he was going to lose Jon James' number.

Then his phone began vibrating.

Jon James.

At first he was definitely going to let it go to voicemail. Then, he got curious. With all that Jon apparently had going on in his day at the moment, what the hell could he possibly be taking the time to call Walker about? He had no idea how much letting his curiosity get the best of him was going to change everything.

Walker answered with a laugh. "I know we really hit it off, but you're coming on a little strong, Jon."

Jon laughed. "Right?" He laughed again. "Though I did have fun almost getting killed outside the gun range with you, this isn't exactly a social call."

Walker stood from the bed and began pacing the room. He knew nothing good could come out of what Jon said next. "All right. I don't really have any work experience, but I'm listening."

"Bullshit, Walker. I'm betting you have just the type of work experience of which I am currently in desperate need."

Walker didn't like the tone, but he did appreciate straight shooting. "What's this about, Jon."

"I saw the way you handled yourself in that parking lot earlier. That was total lack of fear, showing fast-twitch critical thinking, and a high level of skill to turn those men away without so much as a scratch on either one of us. You've been fully trained, and it's more than the basic level I had in the Army. You used to be an operator."

Walker wasn't exactly surprised by Jon's assessment. He was right about everything in the parking lot. No one without training could do that. However, it was the first time that anyone had actually called him out for the secretive work he used to do in his former life and it just sounded odd in his own ears to hear it out loud.

"That's an awfully big leap to make don't you think?" It was all Walker had.

"I don't. It's an easy call for me because I've had a Green Beret working alongside me for over six years."

Walker nodded to himself. "Okay. Suppose what you say is true. I think I've made it very clear that I am retired."

"I know. And Walker, I've probably taken the wrong approach with this so I apologize, I just don't have a lot of time."

"Sounds dangerous," Walker said.

"It's not. Not for a guy like you."

"Then why do you need a guy like me? Go get an off-duty cop. Plenty of those guys picking up jobs on the side for extra money."

Jon was quiet.

Of course, Walker knew why Jon couldn't call an off duty cop. Jon was about to ask him to be a part of something illegal. Something an off-duty cop would have to report. But Walker wasn't going to make it easy for Jon just because Taylor had let him know what was going down.

"I'm going to be honest with you, Walker. Even though I don't know you very well, I can tell what kind of man you are.

A man who knows how to keep private information, well, private. Am I wrong?"

"My entire existence has been based on private," Walker said. Purposefully not directly answering Jon's question.

"I could figure as much. Now, I'm not going to tell you exactly what I've got going down, but let's just say you've met the reason for my current troubles."

"Okay . . ."

"My son, Tate."

Walker didn't need to know the details to understand why his first instincts about Jon were right. He wasn't the one into drugs. It was his dumbass son.

"Let me guess, you need help bailing him out."

Jon cleared his throat. "Well, yes and no. Yes, I do have to bail him out, but only because he dragged me down into the mud with him. And the people he wronged are holding me responsible, because they know I'm the only one of the two of us who can make it right."

"Sounds like a tough situation," Walker said. "But I can't help anyone out who lies to me."

"Excuse me?" Jon scoffed. He did not like the accusation.

"You said you didn't know those men in the parking lot earlier."

Jon laughed. "Oh. Well that's because I don't. Believe me. I wish they were the problem. I wouldn't be bothering you if that were the case."

"So the people Tate wronged are worse that the merry band of boys I dealt with earlier."

"Much, much worse," Jon said without hesitation.

Walker was getting frustrated. "But you just told me what you needed me for wasn't dangerous."

"I know how it sounds. And this one thing tonight isn't dangerous."

"Yet you need the help of who you think might be a trained killer?"

Jon was quiet again.

Walker had paced his way into the living room. He was staring out the window, the intracoastal waters glistened in the evening sun.

"Maybe this was a mistake," Jon said. "I apologize for overreaching."

"No apology needed. Hope you get out of whatever your boy has gotten you into."

Jon sighed. "Gonna take a lot more than hope."

The call ended.

What Jon was into sounded a whole lot more dangerous than what Taylor had made this evening's meetup out to be. She may know what her intentions are, but she needed to know that Jon was trying to hire a certain set of very violent skills. He dialed her number.

"Hey Walker," she answered. "Everything okay?"

"We need to talk."

Taylor laughed. "Well it's a good thing we are on a phone call then, right?"

"Face to face, Taylor."

"Walker, I told you I can't see you tonight, all right? I'm working right now."

"This isn't about me and you. This is about Jon James and what's going on tonight."

"Listen, I have already said too much to you about what is going on with him, all right? You aren't involved in any of this."

"I am now. Jon called me," Walker said.

"Okay, isn't he kinda your friend?"

"He called me about tonight."

"What?"

"Yeah. Where are you?"

"Um, we have a temporary office in the Snell Arcade downtown. I'm here with another agent working on details."

Walker didn't say anything.

"Come down. We're in suite 232. Street parking out front. Is everything okay?"

"Okay with me, I just want to make sure everything is okay with your operation. The devil is in the details, right?"

"Right. See you in a bit, then?"

"I'll be there in thirty."

CHAPTER FIFTEEN

The sun was beginning its slow decent toward the ocean in the rearview of Walker's Mustang. It was still early for downtown, but the food enthusiasts were beginning to fill the streets, and the almost overwhelming amount of dining establishments. Central avenue boasted dozens of bars and restaurants on its own, much less the rest of downtown St. Petersburg.

The GPS on Walker's phone told him he was approaching Fourth Street. He began his scan for a parking spot and noticed a metered one had just opened up in front of the nine story building. It looked like it had been built in a different time. The accents on the stone had actual artisanal qualities in their design. A design that led up to a bell tower atop the structure.

Walker just beat another vehicle searching for a spot as he pulled in and shut off his engine. The sidewalks were busy. A lot of people going in and out of the shops that made up the first floor of the building. When he got out, he noticed Taylor leaning against the wall, hand on her hip, smiling. He walked over.

"Be honest," she said. "This is all just a ploy to see me again, isn't it?"

He leaned in and gave her a kiss. "Yes," he laughed. "You been waiting out here long?"

"Not waiting, just needed some air."

"Going that well is it?"

Taylor shaded her eyes. "Can we walk?"

Walker held out his hand. She took it. "Of course."

They walked without saying a word for a couple of minutes. A warm ocean breeze went with them. Walker just stayed quiet. He could tell Taylor just needed a minute. They covered a few blocks just strolling hand in hand. Up ahead Walker could see the water. Boats lined along a boardwalk on the right side that disappeared behind Pioneer Park.

"No matter what you have to tell me," Taylor said, "I'm glad you came."

Walker dropped her hand and put his left arm around her. He gave her a squeeze. "Everything okay?"

She looked up at him. "No. Our informant got himself arrested in Orlando this morning."

Walker stopped and turned to face her. "So the operation is off?"

Taylor hung her head. "Bosses want us to carry on. Since we told them our informant doesn't personally do runs of his own, they said Jon James wouldn't know the difference if we had a stand in."

"You were just going to do surveillance weren't you?"

She looked up at him. "How would you know that?"

"I've been doing things like this for a long time, Taylor. FBI, or CIA, they don't want the small fish. They trap the small fish to get to the big fish."

"Well, they're worried Jon has stepped up to the big leagues. Some of our intel suggests as much."

Walker couldn't help but shake his head. It was a reflex. Intel was such a subjective thing. It was only as good as the people gathering it.

"What?" she said. "You said you know something. What is it? You still don't think he's into drugs?"

"He is. But . . . It's only because of his son."

"I don't understand. Start from the beginning."

Walker took her hand and stepped over to a nearby park bench. They both had a seat.

"Jon called me. He wanted my help with what was happening tonight."

"Your help? Why would he ever ask a stranger to be involved in something criminal? It could expose him."

"I told you, we had a good rapport. And he could tell that I had skills beyond those of a normal soldier, or federal agent of some kind."

"I don't understand. He doesn't have people like that surrounding him?"

"He does," Walker said, "just not like you and the FBI believes. At least that's how he made it seem."

"Okay," Taylor said. "So, how would having you around help him with a small-time weapons swap?"

"He's worried it could possibly be more than that with this guy being a first-time client. And he's short on help."

"All right. But help with what, Walker? What does he think you are going to help do? Negotiate a better deal? Investigate the boat while the deal is going on? What?"

"He's worried it might get violent, and he wants to be prepared for that."

Taylor looked away. She watched an elderly couple make their way into the park's entrance. Then back to Walker's eyes.

"Is that what you do, Walker? Violence?"

He just continued to look into her eyes. He knew she knew the answer by then, but he still didn't want to say it.

She filled the silence. "Is that why it was so easy for you to step in and take down those men at Caddy's? And why you got the best of Tate's friends in the parking lot earlier?"

She wasn't going to let him off the hook.

But he wasn't about to lie.

"Yes, Taylor," he said. "Violence is quite literally the only thing I've ever known."

Her reaction surprised him.

Taylor reached her hand up to Walker's jaw and caressed his stubbled skin. "You don't have to be that man any more. You don't have to let people keep dragging you back to that place. Not if you don't want to."

Walker took a second. He wasn't sure how to respond because he knew she didn't understand. Hell, he didn't understand it either, it's just who he is. You don't tell an artist to be an accountant. You can't expect a football player to know how to hit a baseball. But you can take what someone made you learn, no matter how bad it is, and make it good. And that is all he was trying to do.

Walker reached up and took her hand. "I appreciate you saying that, and you're absolutely right. I don't have to be that man. But it's who I want to be, Taylor. The difference for me now is how I use what they made me learn. Now I can use it for good. And that's all I'm trying to do."

Taylor leaned in and kissed him. For a moment the world faded away. Like her lips had pulled his being into the wind and everything he'd every done had floated away with it. There had never been another thing in his life that had made him feel so light. So . . . unburdened. And it absolutely terrified him.

Walker pulled away. The weight of the world flooded back to him.

"Did I do something wrong?" Taylor said.

"You haven't had a lot of field experience have you?"

Walker retreated entirely from the overwhelming feelings Taylor had forced on him.

Taylor scooted away from him a bit and cleared her throat. "Um, okay . . . No, I don't have a lot of experience."

Walker could tell he hurt her feelings. He couldn't deal with his own feelings, much less hers. He was no good at relating to anyone, much less a beautiful woman who could melt his pain away. That's too much power for a person to have over him.

"Then I'm doing this with you," Walker said.

"What?"

"I'm going to the drop arranged with Jon, with you. I can keep you safe."

"Walker, I don't need you to keep me safe. That isn't the quality in you that I see. I can take care of myself." Taylor stood. "Thank you for your concern. And thank you for relaying the situation with Jon. It's very helpful. I'll make sure my boss knows it could be more dangerous. I'm sure they'll find someone to tag along with us."

Walker stood. "I didn't mean to offend you."

"I'm not offended. Like I said, I appreciate your help."

"You need someone like me with you. Whether it's me or not."

"Okay, Walker. I hear you. I'll manage. I have done okay so far without you, you know?"

Walker's words weren't landing the way he was intending. "I didn't mean to imply—"

"It's fine. Let's just take a little cool off time, okay? I have to handle this situation. It needs my full concentration."

Walker knew she was saying get lost. It didn't feel so good.

"I understand," he said. "Sorry if I overstepped. Really."

"It's okay." Taylor started to step away. "I do need to go though."

Walker wanted to walk her back, but he at least caught the drift that she wanted to be alone.

So he left her alone.

CHAPTER SIXTEEN

There was a little foot traffic out on the small marina just outside of the abandoned Sea Hags restaurant. Jon stood beside the bar and gazed out the window on the back wall. For the snowbirds who mostly occupied the marina, it wasn't quite snowbird season. But a few older couples were shuffling about. Some carrying fishing gear, others with their coolers. All the traffic that was around now was coming back in. The sun was setting and the water with older eyes wasn't the safest place to be.

Jon was currently taking a little smoke break. The clouds from his cigarette made up most of what he could smell around him, but before he lit up, he could still smell that old fried food scent lingering around the restaurant. He supposed when a restaurant had been open for such a long time, it was probably embedded into the walls.

Jon and Mark had been discussing how things might go later. Three in the morning had been the designated time. His contact that Bud had given him had already pushed off the drop to someone else in his organization. It was a small transaction after all, but it made Jon even more nervous. He would have done the same thing if in the other man's shoes, Jon rarely went to drops himself unless they were of the larger variety. But this was an exception. He couldn't let anything else associated with Vasquez and the Jaurez Cartel be handled by anyone else. Tate had at least taught him that much.

"You're overthinking this one, Jon."

Jon turned from the window. Mark was still sitting quietly at one of the few high-top tables that remained just beyond the bar.

"Yeah? Well, being in debt to one of the deadliest cartels in the world can make a man a bit . . . jumpy."

"You should just let me put together a team to go and take care of the cartel boss. You know, kill the head and the body's dead."

Jon ashed his cigarette out on the bar top then walked over to the table. "You know I love you, Mark, but walking into a cartel den to kill the boss is suicide. It would take you years to do it the right way. Infiltrate from within. That's the only way you can take out a man like Javier Vasquez."

"You see," Mark said, "I don't try to tell you how to sell large quantities of weapons to buyers all over the world, so why do you think you know what it takes to do my job?"

"That sort of thing is a little harder without US intelligence, and more important, the government's pocket book."

"Yeah, but you already have the weapons. And I could have a place staked out in a week. I don't care how big, or how remote."

Jon roused a crooked smile. "How about I just do a couple of things to pay this son of a bitch back, and you keep me alive while I do."

"Because you know what comes next, Jon. I know you do."

Jon did know. But he didn't want to hear it. He'd spent

enough time chewing on the fact that once he sold so much product for Vasquez that he would want him to do it again. Then again. Until he'd used Jon and his resources up entirely.

Mark changed the subject since Jon obviously was not going to finish the conversation about Vasquez taking his soul. "So when do the drugs arrive from Vasquez?"

"Tomorrow night."

Mark sat forward, resting his elbows on the table. "What's the plan."

"Execute this small weapons swap tonight with Chino, Bud's contact. Make him feel good about doing business with us. Then accept the drugs from Vasquez tomorrow night. Then get Chino and his men back down here the night after that to take them off our hands. That's it."

"Jon," Mark said.

"Mark."

"You just going to ignore what we both already know?"

Jon folded his arms. "I'm not going to let Vasquez get his hooks into us."

"You think you have a choice?"

Jon was getting frustrated. "I don't know, Mark. I suppose I'll cross that bridge when I come to it. Fight him if I have to. You think this is the situation that I wanted to be in? I don't want to sell drugs. I'm a weapons man. But I fucked up and let my stupid-ass son run the deal and now here we are."

Mark stood from his seat and held out his arms in a "pump the brakes" sort of way. "Jon, I'm not trying to pour salt in the wound. But I'm a part of this too. Like it or not. And trust me, I do not like it. So I am just trying to make sure all the information is out on the table, and we all know exactly what is going on here. Okay?"

Jon's shoulder's dropped. "I know. And I'm sorry. I never meant for any of this to happen. Just know, Mark, that I'm going to do everything I can to allow us to walk away from this deal. And then maybe we just walk away forever."

Mark nodded. "Maybe that's the best move. Get through these next three days, then disappear for a while. All of us."

"That may not be such a good idea."

Jon reached for the pistol on his hip as he and Mark turned toward the Hispanic accent coming from the adjacent dining room.

The bald headed man in a loud Versace-type patterned shirt held up his hands. "Now, now. I come in peace."

"Who the hell are you?" Jon barked.

"Diego Martinez. Señor Vasquez sent me and his nephew Kaypo here."

Jon took a step to his left so he could see around the wall. A stocky Hispanic man with jet black hair pulled into a ponytail was standing to Diego's right. Neither of them were armed.

"Both of you can just turn around and go back the way you came. We don't need any help here."

"Really?" Diego took a few steps forward. He had a scar that ran vertically down his right cheek. "I've been told that help is exactly what you need. That is why we are all in this mess in the first place, no?"

Jon didn't respond. He took a beat, understanding that since the last deal went sour, it was only natural that Vasquez would want someone from his cartel to keep an eye on things this time around. Jon hated it, but he would have done the same.

"I can't be seen with cartel members, Mr. Martinez. You understand that would be highly detrimental to what we are doing for Vasquez, and my future operations."

"Call me Diego, Jon. And just so we are clear, it doesn't matter at all what you do or don't understand, or what you do and don't want."

"You've got a lot of balls walking in here and saying that," Mark said.

"And you are?"

"Me?" Mark pointed to himself. "I'm the guy who decides if you live or die."

Diego looked from Mark back to Jon. Jon let what Mark said linger for a moment. He wanted to see exactly how Diego would react. Unfortunately, he had no reaction at all. That was the worst kind. Because Diego felt safe. Even on Jon's turf. That meant he knew he was untouchable. Not to mention Vazquez sent family in his nephew? This was bad.

"This how you feel, Jon?"

Jon shook his head. "You're welcome here, Diego. You and your Kaypo. But you won't be involved. In fact, you won't even be seen. It's best for all of us going forward."

Diego smiled and nodded. "I like you Jon. Straight forward, but amicable. Good qualities. Your friend here could learn a lesson."

Mark stepped forward but Jon put his arm out to stop him.

Mark gave Jon a long look. Green Berets aren't good at sitting back. Jon knew it. But this is the way it would have to be. Mark finally took a step back.

"Good boy, Mark." Diego said. Then he looked at Jon. "Make sure you keep him on that leash."

"3:00am," Jon said. "Be here early and you can watch from in here. If you're late, don't come at all."

"I'll let Señor Vasquez know we were welcomed with open arms."

The two of them turned and walked back out the front of the restaurant. Mark picked up the chair beside him and heaved it agains the wall. It shattered into a dozen pieces.

"You done?" Jon said.

"You just going to let him talk to us like that? Like he owns us?"

Jon shook his head. "Mark, I'm going to let him think whatever the hell he wants to think. So he can tell Vasquez all is good. I don't want them here, but this changes nothing. Understand? We execute what we talked about, then we get the hell out of this mess."

Mark didn't speak.

Jon continued. "If anything happens to them, we have a world of problems that there is no need to have. Make sense?"

Mark kicked at one of the broken legs of the chair he'd just shattered. "I hear you. I don't like it. But I hear you."

"I don't like any of this shit. But here we are. Now lets just do whatever it takes to get out of it, and that starts tonight."

CHAPTER SEVENTEEN

As the sun disappeared outside the wall of windows in Walker's rented condo, St. Pete Beach began to relax into a quiet evening. Walker, however, was anything but relaxed. He hadn't stopped pacing the floor since he'd made it back from his visit with Taylor. He'd already cleaned his guns, loaded his spare magazines, and even did a deep clean of the master bathroom. There was no way he could sit down long enough to read a book, so he paced.

His mind wouldn't let him rest. It was as if his operator brain had been ignited by Jon's call earlier. When that happened back when he was on assignments, there was no shutting it off until the deed was done. But now he had no deed. He couldn't help Jon do something illegal, and Taylor said he couldn't help keep her safe while she presided over Jon's illegal activities. It was gut wrenching.

Contrary to what Taylor might have thought, Walker's attempt to help wasn't that he thought he could do her job any better than she could. He just knew that if shit went sideways, he was one of the most qualified people in the world to help get her through it. It had been his entire existence. Nearly two-decades of full immersion. And now he was relegated to a condo that might as well be a cage for a lion that can see its prey just beyond the bars.

There was a flame burning in him now. He didn't think there was any way he could put it out. Not without actually getting out and doing something. But what the hell could he do? He wasn't going to call Jon back. He wasn't going to bother Taylor again. And he had no idea where what was going down later that night was actually going down.

Walker stopped pacing for the first time in over twenty minutes.

The envelope he'd seen in Jon's Ford Bronco flashed into his mind.

9555 Blind Pass Rd.

Walker rushed over to his cell phone and opened the maps app. When he typed in the address, he didn't have to do any investigating. The address was literally right beside him, and it came up labeled as Sea Hags Bar & Grill. Walker didn't have a whole lot of beliefs or superstitions in life, but one thing he always held as true was that there are no coincidences. Whether that be a physical or spiritual belief, didn't really matter to Walker. He just knew that sometimes, as in the case of seeing that address on Jon's envelope, things happen for a reason. And for whatever reason, he was meant to see that address. He could feel it in his bones.

He rushed over to the window that overlooked the abandoned restaurant. There were two parking lots, a dozen tennis courts, and a lot of trees disguising the old building by the water. Not to mention total darkness. So the look out the window was more reflex than a discover mission. He could just make out the shadows of the tops of a few of the boats at the marina on the other side of the restaurant thanks to the glow of the street lights on the adjacent bridge.

Nothing else.

Walker's mind was racing. He'd obviously had no time to stake out Sea Hags, so he had no idea what corners, nooks, or crannies would be good to watch from. He couldn't possibly know where his best hidden vantage points would be. And with never having been inside, there was no way to know escape routes, hiding spots or places to set a trap. What he could do, however, was use the bridge to his advantage.

It was still early. He could get some decent intel from driving, and walking the bridge. Both only once. But he could inconspicuously video and snap pictures. Then he could at least have a small amount of familiarity, if he was actually going to go down there.

Was he?

Walker stared out into the night, but what was in front of him faded away. He could only see his mind's eye. It was filled with Taylor's face, and then the possible dangers all around her. If Jon was looking for a man who could use a gun, then he thought there was a chance guns would be used. That meant Walker would have to be there. Somewhere nearby. Just in case.

Walker went over to the kitchen counter and grabbed his Sig Sauer in its concealed hip holster and strapped it down the front of his jeans. He had two spare magazines in the car's glove box. He threw the strap of the AR-15 scabbard over his shoulder, grabbed his keys, and headed out the door. It was only 10:00pm. He knew that more than likely the drop would happen in the middle of the night, but he wanted to gather as much information as he could. And he wanted to be ready in case something went down earlier than he expected.

Walker stepped outside into the humid night air and his phone began vibrating in his pocket. He fished it out—it was Tim Lawson.

"Hey, Tim."

"Hey there buddy. I'm not interrupting a hot date am I?"

Walker laughed. He hadn't realized he was holding tension in his shoulders, but hearing his friend's voice let them relax. "I wish. But I have had a couple of those lately."

"Good deal. Glad to hear you're doing okay down there in Florida. Not getting into any trouble are you?"

Walker unlocked the trunk of his car and stared at his AR-15 as he put it inside. "Well, the forecast for trouble is actually pretty good for this evening."

"Uh-oh. Suppose you decided to find trouble anyway?"

Walker shut the trunk and opened his door. "Trouble found me if you can believe it."

"I believe it," Tim said. "You're gonna be okay though, right?"

"It's turned out that way so far when trouble has come along."

"Keep it that way, would you?"

"I'll do my best. Everything okay your way?"

Tim laughed. "If I was any better I'd be twins."

Walker laughed with him. "Not really sure what that means, but it sounds good."

"It is. Stay focused out there now. And be safe. Call me tomorrow so I know you're all right."

"Will do. Thanks for checking in. Talk soon."

Walker ended the call and started his car. Even though he knew Taylor would be upset with him for sticking his nose where it didn't belong, he knew that doing this wasn't all about her. He obviously wanted to keep her safe. She had left quite an impression on Walker in the small amount of time that he'd known her. But a lot of this was about him. His need to make sure someone he liked was going to be okay. Right or wrong, that's what it was about. Because he didn't have a whole lot of people he cared about in his life, so he was going to make sure the ones he did stayed safe.

No matter what happened that night, he knew he wasn't going to be sorry for butting in. Even if all that meant was that he watched from afar. And though he never did mind using what he knew to help, he did hope that watching was all he was going to have to do.

CHAPTER EIGHTEEN

Walker felt tired. The adrenaline of staking out Sea Hags for a couple of hours had worn off now that he'd been lying in the back of a random pickup truck bed for about three hours. The aluminum was a far cry from comfortable. And he was thirsty. A stakeout pro he was not.

After driving the bridge slowly once, then walking it even slower, he had spotted a grand total of zero people lurking around. His time in the pickup truck had been a little more fruitful. He'd seen a total of four people in and around Sea Hags. But it had been too dark to spot any discernible features.

After walking the bridge that ran alongside the Sea Hags property, he found a way to hop the rail before the drop from the bridge became too steep. He was able to sneak behind a jet-ski rental tiki hut, then on some pavement there was a pickup truck sitting just thirty yards from the restaurant. There had been minimal boat traffic on the surrounding water, and even less in and around the marina.

The only thing Walker knew about Taylor's rendezvous was that they would be coming in by boat. His vantage point of the marina right outside the restaurant was currently good, but when he heard them coming in, he was going to have to be closer.

Speak of the devil . . .

Walker sat up a little higher when he heard the motor of a boat off in the distance. He keened his ears. After a few seconds, it definitely sounded like it was getting closer. He checked the clock on his phone. 3:05. When he poked his head up over the side rail, he could see two men standing out front now. From his conversation with Jon, he could only assume it was Jon and his Green Beret comrade.

Walker shuffled over to the side of the truck farthest away from the restaurant. He grabbed his AR-15 out of its scabbard and slung it around his neck before he hopped over the side. The sound of the boat grew louder. This was definitely it. Through the passenger window of the pickup truck he could still see the men out front. One of them had moved under the marina light shining down from Sea Hags and he had the same salt and pepper colored crew cut as Jon James.

Walker already knew where he wanted to move. There was a patio on this side of the restaurant that overlooked the marina. The tables and chairs were still there. They would make for good cover in the dark. There was only one door coming out of the restaurant onto the patio. It was the only thing he would have to keep an eye on on the restaurant side. Somewhere, probably inside, were two more men. Walker hadn't seen them in quite some time.

When he was sure Jon's back was turned, Walker sprinted around the front of the truck and sidled up to Sea Hag's outside wall. He slinked along that wall until the patio opened up. Then he ducked down behind the first table in front of him. Now he was close. Jon wasn't more than twenty-five feet diagonally in front of him.

Walker heard Jon speak for the first time. "Your man ready?" Jon said to Mark.

"In position," Mark replied.

The boat was getting closer. Walker could picture Taylor on the boat. He knew she would be nervous. This was going to get very tricky for Walker, and he knew it. He was risking whatever he and Taylor had going on with his presence alone. As new as it was, he definitely felt a connection with her. But no matter how much he enjoyed her, helping her stay safe was far more important to him.

Mark spoke again, "The boat is entering the marina. Stay sharp."

Walker checked the glass door to his right that led back into the restaurant. He didn't see any movement so he duck-walked over to the wooden picket fence that separated the patio from the sidewalk by the water. He could tell that Jon and Mark were talking, but he couldn't hear them any longer over the boat that was pulling in. All he could do was watch.

Movement caught Walker's eye on his right. There were two more men inside the restaurant. He could see them from the light the incoming boat was shining toward Sea Hags. Walker was exposed, but if he moved, they might see him. Right now, their attention was focused forward, through the windows that overlooked the marina. Both of them had guns in their hands. Mark had radioed to someone to be ready just a moment ago. Walker could only assume it was these two men. And he could only hope the guns were just a precaution. Just in case, Walker slid his Sig Sauer from its holster.

Back outside, there were bags being exchanged. From what Taylor had said, it was the weapons Jon was selling. The bag from the boat must be FBI money. Then he saw her. The light shined just right on the inside of the boat and Taylor's golden hair sparkled. The big man on the boat tossed out the duffel bag as Jon's man, Mark, handed over two large hard cases one by one. Walker still couldn't hear what was being said over the idling boat, but it looked as though the exchange was going fairly smooth.

Then all hell broke loose.

Sirens sounded from the parking lot behind him. Walker watched the man on the boat cut the rope and just as it began to pull away from the dock there were gunshots. Walker obviously didn't know what Taylor's plan had been with this operation, but he did know that someone had made a mistake and fired up the sirens too soon. There was just no reason for it. All they induced was Jon having to fight his way out of a situation that didn't need a fight.

Walker watched as Mark pulled Jon behind one of the metal storage containers that sat at the water's edge. Two shadows surprised everyone at the left side of the dock, but they disappeared into the water just as quickly when the two men inside the restaurant fired on them.

"No!," Jon shouted from the dock. "Stop shooting!"

Walker didn't know exactly what was going on, but it was clear in that moment that the two men inside the restaurant were not taking orders from Jon. Walker moved over to the door. He had a shot at the men as they were moving around the bar, but he didn't take it. He had no role there. Instead, he followed behind them, into the restaurant, then around the bar. He was hoping Taylor's team would catch them before anyone else got hurt. After the already botched play, however, Walker held little hope.

Taylor's boat was at full throttle. He could hear the engine roaring as it moved between the boats in the marina. Walker stopped short of the door the two Hispanic men ran onto the dock from. He looked to his left. Jon and Mark were just getting to their feet.

"Just let them go!" Jon shouted in the direction of the

Hispanic men who were racing down one of the boat ramps on the right.

The men were making a run for a boat. That meant they were going after Taylor. He should have shot them down when he had the chance. He knew better than to go against his instincts. He just wasn't used to working in the confines of having other people involved. Now, he couldn't just stand there and let them put her in danger. But he didn't have any experience driving a boat. He doubted he would even know how to get one started. So he did the only thing he could and stepped out onto the dock. He did so with his gun pointed in Jon and Mark's direction. The light shining down from the outside wall of Sea Hags lit all three of them.

"Who the hell are you?" Mark said as he moved his gun onto Walker. "Put the gun down or I'll shoot!"

"Walker?" Jon said.

"No time to explain, Jon. I just can't let those men get to that other boat."

"They aren't my men, Walker. I can't control them. But what the hell are you doing here?"

A boat engine fired up. The Hispanic men were getting away.

Two shadows moved around the corner of Sea Hags, behind Jon and Mark, from the direction Walker had been watching them from. "Drop your weapons!" A man shouted. "Now! Or we'll shoot!"

Walker didn't have time for more explaining to Jon, and he certainly didn't have time to get interrogated by Taylor's FBI team. The Hispanic men were clearly making a move to stop everyone on Taylor's boat. They wouldn't have fired on them in the first place if that weren't the case. So the only thing Walker cared about in that moment was stopping them. If he got shot in the process, well, at least he tried.

Walker moved his pistol from Jon and Mark, to the left,

just in front of the man who'd shouted at them a moment ago. Walker could just see them behind the wooden fence that separated them from the dock. He fired twice at the right edge of the fence, making sure he wouldn't hit anyone. The he turned and sprinted down the same ramp the Hispanic men had taken. Since he couldn't captain a boat himself, he was going to have to make it to the boat they were taking before they could get it out of the marina.

There was shouting behind him. He ducked his head as he ran away, as if somehow that would make him harder to hit if they opened fire. About six boats ahead he could see one of them moving backward. That was his ride. Now he had to get on board no matter what it took, and worry about the two gunmen after the fact.

One problem at a time.

CHAPTER NINETEEN

The boat the Hispanic men were pulling out of the marina had fully backed out of its space. Walker could hear the throttle move from reverse to forward just as he leapt onto the boat that had been parked beside it. There was just enough light from the boat ramp to see the cushion he landed on, and the top of the motor at the back of the boat. He had no choice but to use it as a springboard. When he planted his right foot on top of the motor, it didn't react the way he'd hoped it would. Instead of getting a huge boost—enough to propel him onto the boat that was now pulling away—the motor sank under his weight and Walker fell face-first into the ocean. The boat with the two men who had been shooting at Taylor sped away into the night.

Walker waded in the water for a moment, looking all around him, searching for a way to go after them. He'd never felt so hopeless than he did watching that boat leave after Taylor. His feelings for her were even deeper than he'd thought. Now he had no way to get to her. Ironically, he was a fish out of water when it came to the ocean and its modes of transportation. Along with the wake of the boat that had just sped away, a sinking feeling washed over him.

He wasn't going to be able to save her.

Then another boat engine roared to life. Walker turned in the water, through the burning salt water in his eyes he looked back toward Sea Hags. A boat quickly backed out away from the ramp. As soon as it was facing him, it began moving forward. As the boat grew closer, he could see an arm reach out over the white of its side. On reflex, he reached up and grabbed it. When he was up over the side, he was staring Jon in the face. Mark was driving the boat.

"Why are you helping me?" Walker said, drenched in water he shook like a wet dog.

"Because you are going to help me."

Mark had yet to throttle forward. Jon nodded back over Walker's shoulder toward the dock. Three shadows had gathered there. One of them was yelling, but it wasn't intelligible. Walker looked back at Jon.

"Right?" Jon said. "These are your people. Your a Fed right? You can help get me out of this if I help you?"

There was desperation in Jon's eyes.

Walker didn't want to lie to him. However, his desire to help Taylor far outweighed his moral code at the moment. So he nodded. Jon looked back over his shoulder and nodded to Mark. Walker had to grab the seat beside him to keep from falling when the boat launched forward.

The air in St. Pete Beach was warm. Probably around eighty degrees. But when there was no sun and he was drenched with ocean water, Walker had quite a chill. He wiped the salt water from his face with his hands. Which were little use. Then he pulled his AR from its scabbard and racked the charging handle. Mark steered the boat right out of the marina toward the open intracoastal waterway.

"You see them?" Mark shouted from the captain's chair as he slowed the boat.

After they rounded the marina they could go left or right into the intracoastal. Walker jumped up from his seat and looked left. He didn't see anything.

"There!" Jon shouted from the starboard side of the boat.

Walker rushed over. He could just see a red light shining off the back of a boat. Just as he made it to the rail, Mark went full throttle as he turned to the right. Walker didn't know much about anything when it came to boating, but he had overheard a few of the older men by the pool talking about how shallow parts of the intracoastal could be. As shallow as four feet.

"Make sure you watch the depth finder!" Jon shouted over the roar of the engine and the spray of the water.

Walker had to let them worry about the boat. He readied what he was good at. His weapon. And he sat by the rail, ready for whatever came next. But what came was a lot of bumpy water. The wind had picked up considerably as the night moved into morning. Walker was doing his best not to get tossed to the floor. Jon took a seat beside him.

"We can deal with why the hell you lied to me about what you do later. What the hell are you going to do now?"

"Who are those men?" Walker shouted back.

Jon turned and looked toward the boat. They were gaining on it, but it was taking longer than Walker had hoped. Jon looked back. "Now's not the time. I need to explain this entire thing. I just need to know what I have to do to keep myself out of prison long enough to get this monkey off my back."

Walker had to keep Jon believing he could help him, at least until Taylor was safe. So he just played along. "If you have a good explanation for all this, you'll be fine if you just get me close enough so that I can stop those men from hurting my people!"

Jon nodded. They were drawing close to the boat. "You just have to promise me one thing, Walker—if that is your real name. You can't kill these guys. Under no circumstance. You hear me? I can explain why, later. But you have to promise me that!"

Walker did hear him. But there was no way he could keep a promise like that. Not with Taylor's life in danger.

"Deal," Walker said anyway.

"I need to hear you say it, Walker!"

"I promise for God's sake! Now just get me to that boat!"

Before Walker could understand what was happening, he and Jon were both thrown to the deck. Mark had throttled down so fast there was no way they could stay in their seats. Walker looked up at Mark, but before words could be exchanged, he heard gunshots. Walker scrambled to the front of the boat. In front of him was what looked like condos. Each of them had a deck, and below it an open garage, but not for cars. There were boats docked beneath them. Single boat slips. Each of the decks, six in total stretched one after another on the left side, had bright lights shining down over the water.

The lights revealed a small marina of boats. Only three rows of six. In the distance between the condos and the boat ramps was just enough water room to turn a boat around. That's where Walker saw Taylor's boat about thirty yards inside of it, with no where to turn around, because the two Hispanic men had their boat blocking the exit. They were firing at Taylor's boat. No return fire that Walker could see.

What he could see was the silhouette of one of the Hispanic men standing on the back of their boat, firing his weapon. Walker stood, bending his knees to keep his balance on the wavering bow. He swung his AR into firing position.

"He said you can't shoot them!" a man shouted from behind Walker.

Just as Walker was squeezing the trigger, he felt a blow to his back. The round he'd fired sank into the water just off the bow, and so did he as he toppled over the rail. As he came up out of the water, he turned back toward the boat and raised his gun as he kicked to stay afloat. Mark was standing over him holding a pistol.

"What the hell are you doing?" Jon shouted as he ran up. Gunshots continued behind Walker.

Mark answered by raising his gun and pointing it down at Walker.

"Mark!" Jon shouted as he pounded down on Mark's arm with his fist. It saved Walker's life. The bullet he fired missed because Jon had hit him.

Walker prepared to shoot, but Jon had grabbed Mark and they were fighting. He didn't have time to wait around and see the end of the skirmish, Taylor was in trouble. He let his AR float from the sling around his neck and used both arms to swim for the boat the Hispanic men were firing from. There was no way he could tell if Taylor was okay or not. But the longer they had to fill her boat with bullets, the worst her chances would be.

CHAPTER TWENTY

THE WATER BENEATH HIM WAS AS BLACK AS THE SKY ABOVE. Heavy clouds had rolled in. For some reason, as Walker swam madly toward the boat that held the two men firing shots at Taylor, the image of the front page of the local paper sitting on a table in the workout room with the headline, *The Storm Is Coming,* flashed in his mind. Walker didn't have further information about any inclement weather, but the storm that mattered most had already made it to St. Pete Beach, and it was raining bullets.

Walker pushed Mark and Jon's fight in the boat behind him from his thoughts. He focused solely on the rail of the 28-foot, center console fishing boat just above him. He kicked his legs with power and it propelled him high enough to get a handhold on the chrome rail. He gripped with both hands now and pulled himself high enough to swing a stabilizing leg over the rail. He reached down to his AR, found the handle, then brought it up and squeezed the trigger. The man with his back to him fell forward off the boat and into the water.

Walker moved his gun toward the second man but before

he could shoot, the man dove in over the side. Walker pulled himself fully over the side and stood. As he moved around the center console he raised his gun to shoot the man swimming for shore. But before he could fire, bullets pelted the center console that was at his back. Walker spun, but had to duck when more bullets came. It was too dark to see if it was Mark or Jon shooting at him, but ultimately it didn't matter. He had to retaliate to save his own life.

Walker fired back at Jon's boat. The shadowy figure ducked for cover as well. Walker looked over his shoulder toward Taylor's boat about thirty feet away, it was rubbing against the wall of one of the condos. He couldn't see anyone on board.

"Taylor!" he shouted. "Taylor, are you all right?"

More gunfire from Jon's boat. Walker angled around the captain's chair at the center of the boat. Either Jon or Mark was doing the same on their boat. Walker had to assume Jon was the one he couldn't see. The way Jon described Mark—a Green Beret—Jon wouldn't have stood a chance in the fight. Walker didn't have time to worry about what that meant for Jon, or what was really going on inside their fold, he just had to get out of there so he could help Taylor.

Walker had worked with Green Beret's before. They were the real deal. So first things first, he'd have to survive Mark.

"Taylor!" he shouted again.

Nothing.

He took a long breath to steady himself. Then he tried a new approach.

"Mark?"

He wasn't responding either. Walker continued.

"I don't care what's going on between you and Jon, Mark. That's your business. I'm not a Fed like he thinks I am. I just want to help my friend. She's on the boat that the guys you are working with were shooting at."

"You know Taylor?" a man's voice shouted behind him from Taylor's boat.

Walker turned, keeping the center console between him and Mark. "Is she okay?"

"She's unconscious. And bleeding. I think she hit her head when she went down."

"I hate to break up this heartfelt moment," Mark said from his boat. "But you stepped in some real shit here."

"I'm assuming you're talking to me?" Walker said.

"Jon got in over his head," Mark said. " He let his moron son run a mission I should have been running. He pissed off the people you can't afford to piss off."

"Can't afford to piss off, how?" Walker said. "Because they turned around and hired you? And now you're going to make Jon pay?"

The water was quiet. There were a few distant sirens. Walker noticed a few lights come on in the surrounding windows, but so far they had been smart enough to stay inside. They would be calling the police. Mark would know they would be there soon.

"Just toss Jon over the side if you haven't killed him, Mark. Then take the boat and get out of here. I don't give a damn about any of this shit. I just want to get my friend some help. And Jon some help if it's not too late."

"Doesn't matter if I let you live," Mark said. "Doesn't matter if I leave now. You all are going to have to die. My boss won't leave unturned stones. Especially now that the federal government is involved."

"I told you," Walker said. "I'm not FBI. I don't work for the government in any form."

"No? Maybe not, but the people on that boat do."

"They haven't seen you," Walker said. "They only know that Jon runs the show."

Everyone was quiet.

"Which one of the men did you shoot?" Mark asked Walker.

"You mean the Hispanic man on this boat?" Walker clarified.

"Yeah. Which one did you shoot?"

"I don't have time for this, Mark. My friend might be dying. And if she dies, so do you."

Walker heard Mark laughing. Walker felt his hand tighten around the grip of his gun.

"You have no idea what I'm capable of," Mark said, the laugh still lingered in his words.

"I think it's you who is the ignorant one," Walker said.

"She's not waking up!" the man's voice came back from Taylor's boat. "She needs help!"

Walker felt a bolt of panic strike him.

Walker raised his gun and began firing at Mark. He was tired of the pissing contest. He had to help Taylor. The sirens were getting closer. They would be able to take Taylor to the hospital, but Walker needed to clear the area of danger so they could get her off the boat.

Off to his left, back in the direction of Sea Hags where they had just come from, Walker could now see flashing lights moving over the dark water. He stopped firing.

"If you go now, Mark," Walker shouted. Though he really didn't need to over the still water. "I'll occupy them until you're out of sight. Like I said, I only care about getting my friend some help."

"You fucked up getting involved in this," Mark said. Walker could see him move around the center console. Then the engine started. "Jon needed this deal to go through. Not just to save himself, but his son too."

Walker heard a splash not far from Mark's boat.

"Now they're both dead. And Jon told me your name and where you're staying. So you and your friend are dead too.

And anyone else you know and love if you shot the wrong man a minute ago. That's why I asked which one you shot. If he's got a ponytail, and a tear drop tattoo under his left eye, that's my boss's nephew. His only living family. And you'll never survive that wrath."

The boat engine surged and Mark was gone in a second. Walker glanced up and saw the flashing lights getting closer on the water. He could also see blue and reds bouncing off the walls of one of the condos on land. He knew that if Taylor didn't make it, he was going to prison for a very long time without her to corroborate that he was there helping the good guys. But that was a chance he was going to have to take. Because from Mark's words, from knowing Jon's problems were about drugs, and there being two Mexican men there who were firing at the FBI, Walker had to get all the information he could about what might be coming.

Walker could see that the police had made it to the edge of the water from the condo's parking lot. He'd heard the man who was with Taylor shout, "FBI. We have a gunshot wound". They were going to help Taylor. He needed to know how bad the mess was he'd put himself in. First he rushed over to the side of the boat that had been closest to Mark. He took out his phone. It was still working despite his swim through the ocean. He hit it's flashlight and scanned the water. It first found a shoe. He moved the light up and saw Jon floating face up.

He turned and found a net connected to about a three foot pole. He reached out over the water and managed to get the net over the tip of Jon's shoe. He pulled slowly until he could reach him. Walker grabbed Jon's jeans with his right hand, then his shirt collar with his left, and hauled him up. He laid him on the seat that ran along the inside of the boat. He could hear Jon breathing. He was just unconscious.

Walker left him there and moved to the other side of the boat with the net in his hand.

"Don't move!" a man shouted from shore. "You, on the boat! Stay right there!"

Walker ignored him. The police boat was also pulling up. He didn't need the phone's light on the land side of the boat because the lights from the condo were shining on the man he'd shot as he lay face down in the water. Walker reached over the side. He didn't attempt to pull him in, he just rolled him over.

Under the man's left eye, atop his light brown skin, was a black dot. It was the tear drop Mark had spoken of. Walker knew he'd more than likely killed some important drug cartel member's family. Worst case scenario.

"Drop your weapon and put your hands up!" a man's voice sounded from a bullhorn. It was coming from the direction of the police boat that had pulled up short to assess the situation.

"You heard him! Hands up!" the man from shore shouted again. Two loud claps sounded and Walker saw him fall face-first into the water. Off to the left, Walker saw the Hispanic man who'd jumped from the boat holding a gun beneath a deck light. The man then opened fire on the boat that was just telling Walker to put his hands up.

Walker raised his gun and just as he squeezed the trigger, the boat opened fire beside him and the man dove out of sight. He slammed his fist on the cushion beside him. Other people were definitely not making it easy for him to do what he does. While the police boat beside him was occupied, he had a decision to make. Go after the Hispanic man now, and risk getting shot, or arrested by the police, or let the police do their job and disappear so he could have a chance to protect Taylor tomorrow.

If she was alive.

The decision was easy. No one had seen him enough to be able to finger him. And he had Jon in the boat with him, who, once he woke up, could be a formidable ally in helping Walker sort through the current mess. If Mark was telling the truth, and he did know Walker and where he lived, he and Jon were in a world of trouble. Especially if he had to balance helping Taylor if she pulled through. Walker could see now that the Hispanic man was surrounded. They were going to be able to get Taylor out safely.

There was just one problem. Walker didn't know how to drive the boat. He looked over his shoulder and saw Jon was still unconscious. He'd always wanted to learn. And his asshole foster father had always told him the best way to learn was trial by fire. He was going to have to try. He just hoped he didn't burn both him and Jon alive in that learning fire before he could get them to safety.

CHAPTER TWENTY-ONE

IT TURNED OUT THAT DRIVING THE BOAT ACTUALLY WASN'T all that hard. Turn the key and the boat starts. The push the throttle forward to go forward part, was a little tricky at first because he was used to pushing a pedal down in a car to do the same. But he got the hang of it. Then he just had to use the wheel to turn. He didn't know how to read a depth finder, but he was aware enough to know that when Mark was driving the boat, he was staying close to the marker signs that were in the middle of the intracoastal waterway. Made sense to Walker that he should do the same. The thing that he was happy he didn't have to do was park the boat. That would have been a disaster. And he was glad he didn't have to know where to go, because Jon had woken up just in time to steer them to Jon's house not far from where everything went down.

Before Walker pulled away from the scene, he used his AR-15 to put about twenty rounds in the bottom of the police boat. Just to make sure they couldn't follow him. On land, the road did not run right along the intracoastal, so once he pulled away, there was no following him.

When Jon pulled up to his dock they got off the boat, then Jon put it in reverse and jumped off. The boat managed to make it out of sight before it hit anything. Good for when the cops did go combing for it. Jon had grabbed a towel from his own boat that was docked there and was drying himself off. He tossed Walker one too.

"What about the house?" Walker said. "Won't Mark know to make this the first stop on the hit parade?"

There was a light shining down from a wooden post that hung over the dock. Walker could see hurt in Jon's eyes. It was clear that Mark turning on him had been quite the shock.

"I put Mark up in the Don CeSar Hotel, South of here on the beach. He was like a son, but I've always kept him separate from me personally. He thinks I'm staying in one of the renovated condos in your complex."

Walker thumbed over his shoulder. "Won't this house be in your name? Easy to look up?"

"I bought it under one of my holding companies that he knows nothing about. I've had it for years as an investment property. But I understand your thought process. He's good. He'll eventually find it. But we're okay for a couple of nights."

"You all right?" Walker said.

Jon chuckled. "Physically? Sure . . . for now. Mentally, I'm exhausted. But thanks for pulling me out of the water. Even though it is your fault I ended up there."

"Excuse me?" Walker put his hands on his hips.

"Your team is the reason I am in this mess now. I had a light at the end of the tunnel, and you just pushed a rock slide in front of it."

Walker nodded. "Okay. We ready for a *real* talk then?"

"Some honesty would be nice."

"Honesty goes both ways. Like it or not, we're in this

together now. And for the record, you're the reason I'm in trouble, and the reason my friend is maybe fighting for her life right now. Don't get it twisted, Jon."

"Bullshit. You ruined a perfectly—"

"I'm not a fed, Jon. I'm not CIA. Hell, I'm not even a beat cop. The only reason I showed up tonight was to help my friend. And it's a good thing I did because you might have gotten her killed."

Jon puffed out his chest. "She nearly got *me* killed. Her team botched whatever they were doing all to hell!"

Walker took a step back. "Maybe we should cool off. Take a break and go inside? There's no need for you to lose two fights tonight."

"You think you're man enough to take me? Then try it. See what happens."

"I'm an assassin, Jon."

Walker let that linger in the growing wind that was blowing through the surrounding palm trees. A spark of lightning flashed in the distance. Jon's chest deflated a bit and he crossed his arms over his wet black t-shirt.

Walker continued. "I was trained by the kind of men who trained Mark. And far beyond. Green Berets, Navy SEALs, Marine Snipers, secret agents, Muay Thai and Brazilian Jiu jitsu experts, all to make sure I was the government's, and my program's greatest secret weapon. The universe favored you today when it dragged me into your mess. But now you need to understand that I am not your enemy. I am the dog you let off the leash after you've pointed me in the direction of your enemy."

Jon nodded. "All right." He pointed behind Walker at the house. Let's get inside."

Walker followed behind Jon. His mind was racing on next steps. Being alone to think and plot would have been preferred, but he knew no one in the Tampa Bay area. Zero contacts. He wouldn't even know where they would be taking Taylor. As far as he remembered, he hadn't seen a hospital since he'd been there at all. He didn't want what was happening with her to factor in any of the decisions that had to be made, but he was worried about her. And he was pissed she'd been hurt, but it was a lot of people's fault.

Whoever had told the waiting police or FBI to sound the charge and move in at Sea Hags had put everyone unnecessarily in danger. The two Hispanic men made it worse from there. He wasn't sure how he felt about Jon at the moment but having a Green Beret on the opposite side of the battle was bad. Not because Walker feared him, but because he didn't want to kill a former soldier who'd served his country. But, it certainly wouldn't be the first time.

The air conditioning inside Jon's place gave Walker a chill. He removed the AR scabbard from around his neck and placed it on the counter in Jon's kitchen. Everything in the house was modern. Light tan hardwood floors, white and gray granite countertops, gray walls, and artwork that looked as though it were selected by a museum rather than a man.

"Any idea where they might take my friend?"

"Not sure. I'm not a local either." Jon opened the stainless steel fridge. "Mineral water?"

"I'll take whatever you've got."

"Something stronger then?"

"As long as it's brown."

Jon shut the fridge and opened the adjacent cabinet. "I don't do scotch. Only bourbon. That work?"

"I'm from Kentucky."

Jon whipped around. "No shit? My mom was born and raised in Louisville."

"I'm Eastern Kentucky. Ashland area."

"Not familiar."

Jon set down two glasses and a bottle of Eagle Rare Bourbon.

"Do I even have to ask?" Jon said as he popped the cork.

"Neat."

"Only way to drink it."

Walker watched while Jon poured.

"So," Jon slid a glass over to Walker. "If you don't know anybody in the Tampa area, how the hell do you have a friend in the, well, the FBI, right?"

Walker nodded. He picked up the glass and swirled the bourbon as he brought it to his nose. Caramel, oak, and brown sugar all said hello. He took a sip. He was used to drinking much stronger barrel proof bourbon, but the Eagle Rare did the trick. "Yeah, FBI. And I met her at Caddy's. She hit on me the night before I met your charming son."

Jon rolled his eyes as he sipped. "Two of you must have gotten close, fast. Especially for her to know what you are, and to already have used you for work."

"Remind you of anyone?"

Jon smiled.

"You wanted to use me for work awfully soon yourself," Walker said. "In the end you got your wish."

"Yeah, but I wasn't willing to sleep with you to get something from you."

"Taylor doesn't know what I do. She only assumes. And she had no idea I was there tonight. I'm pretty good at finding trouble without anyone's request."

"How *did* you know where to go then?" Jon finished his drink and poured another. Walker held out his glass for a fill-up. "I never told you about Sea Hags."

"No, but I saw the address on an envelope in your truck. It didn't take Sherlock Holmes to do the rest. Who were those Hispanic men?"

Jon set down his glass and hung his head with a sigh. "A long story that was supposed to be short."

"You're going to have to do better than that," Walker said.

Jon nodded toward the backyard. "Let's get out of this cool air and watch the storm come in."

Walker agreed. "Should you bring the bourbon?"

Jon walked by with the bottle in hand. It was all the answer Walker needed—about how long the story would take, and just how bad the news would be that he was about to get.

The news ended up being a lot worse than he'd ever imagined.

CHAPTER TWENTY-TWO

WALKER SHUT OFF THE ENGINE OF HIS MUSTANG IN THE parking lot of Bayfront Health Hospital. He adjusted his review mirror to see the sunrise, but it was being shadowed by clouds. The news was saying that the hurricane, which had been downgraded to a tropical storm, was making landfall more to the North, in the panhandle around Panama City Beach. The rain in St. Pete was still supposed to reach torrential proportions. He looked out his window and could see the rain in the West. It was coming.

Walker had spent the last hour and a half alone. He'd been doing nothing but soul searching. And he was continuing that search as he sat staring at the hospital in front of him. He listened to Jon's entire story of how he got himself into his current mess. Walker tried to have empathy for him, after all, his intention was never to be in his current situation. But intentions are like goals. If you set a goal, but don't follow any of the steps it takes to reach that goal, that goal was just a dream. And a dream is merely a make-believe wish you whisper to the stars, only hoping it will come true.

Which it won't, if you never set a goal and work the necessary steps to achieve it.

So, whether Jon wanted to be where he is or not, he's there because of his decisions, which were also illegal. What Walker had to decide was if that meant he wasn't worth helping. Hence the soul searching. The other answers he was looking for was laying in a hospital bed in the building in front of him. Walker's next thought was that if he didn't help Jon, what did that mean for Taylor? Someone he really cared about. And an innocent someone that was now in Jon's mess involuntarily. If he didn't help Jon, then he was leaving Taylor to fend for herself. Which, she did make very clear yesterday evening that doing her job on her own was exactly what she wanted.

However, whether she knew it yet or not, Taylor would be dead if Walker had stayed away like she'd insisted. And if Javier Vasquez is even a fraction as ruthless as Jon made him out to be, he and his Juarez Cartel would never let Taylor live. They would tie off every lose end from last night. Including Walker.

That was the last of the soul searching. Walker was already trying to stay hidden from one powerful and merciless organization in his former employer at Maxwell Solutions. Did he really want two monkeys on his back? He knew if he disappeared, there probably wouldn't be a lot of time spent trying to find him. But if Walker did decide to disappear, and then he found out Vasquez had gotten to Taylor, would he be able to live with himself?

No.

She already meant too much to him. He would, of course, hate to hear that Jon had been killed, but he's a grown man who got himself into his situation. Taylor was innocent. And . . . Walker *really* liked her. The soul searching had actually been over before it ever really began. He'd known the answer all along, he supposed he just wanted to settle in his own head the exact reasons he was going to risk his life to help people he barely knew. Now he had.

Walker stepped out of his car. The wind was really blowing now. The palm trees began to look as if they were holding a great invisible weight, bending at the will of mother nature's breath. Walker pulled his ball cap low on his forehead. No one knew him, but for some reason he felt better with a little cover.

About an hour ago, Taylor's team member called Walker's cell phone. He was the same man from her team that had been on the boat with her when she was injured last night. Taylor had regained consciousness. When this same team member told Taylor about the unknown man on the boat last night who'd stopped the shooters, she'd told him to call Walker. He didn't know if that was a good or a bad thing that she knew it was him, but at least he knew she was safe, and she requested that he come and see her.

Walker stepped through the automatic doors to the hospital. He arrived at the exact time he'd said he would, and he knew without knowing that the man walking toward him was FBI. Maybe it was his standard issue, clean cut, dark hair mixed with the navy blue polo and khaki pants, but he could just see the only thing missing was the jacket with the acronym emblazoned in yellow on the back.

"Mr. Walker?"

Walker nodded. The man reached out his hand. Walker shook it.

"Jason Street. I just want to thank you for saving my, and my entire team's asses out on that water."

"I wouldn't have had to if your cover hadn't prematurely been blown by your own people."

The man hung his head. "Yeah. We should have never involved local law enforcement."

"Guess not," Walker said. "How is she?"

"Agent Crenshaw, yes. She's doing good considering the circumstances. Follow me." As he walked, he looked back over his shoulder. "She asked about you twice since I called you. Her head's still a little foggy."

Walker followed Jason to the elevator.

"What happened exactly?" Walker said.

"Pretty bad concussion, but luckily the bullet was easy for the doctor to remove."

"Bullet?"

"Shit, yeah. Sorry. Thought I told you she was shot in the shoulder. Took it like a champ. You wouldn't think someone who looked like her would be so tough."

"You'd be surprised."

Walker didn't know what else to say. Small talk was not his thing. The elevator door opened and they both took a left.

"I didn't know Taylor was seeing anyone," Jason said as they walked.

Walker felt his stomach flip. He didn't know she was seeing anyone either. He liked the way it sounded though. "No?" He played it off.

"No," Jason said. "Guess we don't talk much else but work. I'm glad she has someone. She's one of the good ones."

Walker smiled. Jason kept walking. Walker's mood had lifted a bit. Attention from a beautiful woman has that effect on any red-blooded man.

"Right here," Jason said as he grabbed the handle on the door.

Through the small rectangular window in the door, Walker could see Taylor was sleeping. Her head was turned toward him; eyes closed. He turned back to Jason.

"I'll take it from here," Walker whispered.

Jason nodded, then backed out of the door. Walker

caught the door and made sure it shut softly. He padded over to the chair that sat beside the bed. Somehow, Taylor was even more beautiful lying in that hospital bed, no makeup, no putting on. All of us when our health is failing in someway are reduced to our most vulnerable state. Walker's handler used to always tell him that humans were fools . . . that time and health are the only real currencies on earth. Time you can never get back, and with poor health you can never enjoy the time that's always slipping away.

Walker slipped away as he watched, and listened to Taylor's steady breathing. Then he was asleep.

CHAPTER TWENTY-THREE

Walker felt something squeeze his hand. His eyes popped open and he sat up straight. The he relaxed into a smile when it was Taylor looking over at him.

"Hey there handsome," she said.

Walker scooted his chair closer to the bed, reached up, and tucked a loose strand of blond hair back behind her ear.

"How are you feeling?"

Taylor smiled. "Better now."

Walker took her hand in his. "You had me worried there."

"I'm sorry."

Walker shook his head. "No, don't do that. You have nothing—"

"I should have listened. You tried to tell me and instead of listening I tried to play Miss Independent."

"I don't see it that way at all."

"No?" Taylor said as she sat up a little.

Walker stood and helped her adjust the pillow behind her back. She smiled the thank you this time.

"No," Walker said. "You don't even know me, Taylor. To take advice from me about what you do for a living doesn't even make sense. You did the right thing. It just didn't turn out the way it should have."

"Yeah, I would say not." Taylor looked to her right out the window. Rain had begun dancing on the glass. Gray had overtaken the sky and it looked threatening. Walker let her work slowly into her thoughts. She looked back over at him. "Thank you for coming last night even though I told you not to. Jason said you saved our lives."

"It was a bad situation, made worse by things you couldn't foresee."

"How did you know where we would be?"

"I saw an address on an envelope in Jon's car. I put two and two together. I got lucky."

Taylor laughed, but the laugh turned into a cough. For the first time she pawed at her injured shoulder and winced. "I doubt it had anything to do with luck."

Walker's phone vibrated. It was a message from Jon. When Walker had left Jon's house he'd asked him to message him if Mark reached out. Jon's message said, *Just heard from Mark. I couldn't trust that he would leave Vasquez and come back to me so I told him to go fuck himself. It got heated. He said he was coming for all of us. And Walker, he said he gets a bonus for any government officials. I'm really sorry—*

Walker didn't finish reading the text. A pit formed in his stomach as he searched the room for Taylor's clothes. He must have been wearing the worry on his face.

"What's wrong?" Taylor said.

He looked over, then down at his phone, then back to her. He was going to play it off, but now wasn't the time to mince words.

"How much has Jason told you?"

Taylor sat up straighter and her face grew longer. "I don't like the sound of that. What is it? He hasn't told me anything."

"Taylor . . ." Walker took a second to ponder how to deliver the news. He had always been a Bandaid type of guy. He supposed scaring her wouldn't exactly be a bad thing. It might just be the only way to get her moving.

"Don't sugarcoat it if that's what you're considering," she said. "How bad is it?"

Bandaid it is. "The two men who were chasing after you, and shooting at you—"

"*Shot* me."

"Shot you," Walker went on. "They weren't Jon James' men."

Taylor's eyes widened.

Walker continued. "They were part of the Juarez Cartel—"

"The *Juarez Cartel?*" Taylor's voice rose an octave. "What the hell were they doing there?"

"Long story short, Jon's son, Tate, botched an arms deal with the Juarez Cartel. What's worse is that the Juarez Cartel was loaded up for a drug drop they were going to do after they picked up the weapons. A rival gang intervened and took it all. The only reason the rival gang knew about any of it was because Tate was sleeping with a woman in that rival gang and ran his mouth. Javier Vasquez personally held Jon responsible for Tate's screw up. That's why Jon has to sell the drugs. To get the Juarez Cartel off his back."

"Holy shit," Taylor's mouth slacked open.

"It gets worse."

"Worse?" Taylor folded her arms across her chest. "How could it be worse than having maybe the world's most vicious drug cartel after you?"

"Only one way," Walker said. "Make it personal for Javier Vasquez."

"I don't understand," Taylor said, now wringing her hands.

"One of the two men Vasquez sent to watch over Jon was his nephew."

"No."

"And I shot and killed him last night to keep him from killing you."

"Oh my god."

They both sat there as the weight of the situation moved over them like the dark clouds rolling just outside the window. Walker had obviously known that the situation was terrible, but for some reason saying it out loud to Taylor really helped it sink in.

"There's more," Walker said.

Taylor closed her eyes and let her head fall back against the pillow. Even though she had to, she didn't want to hear it. "Well, don't stop now."

"Jon's right hand man, Mark, he . . ." Walker went quiet. Taylor sat up. "He had strongly advised Jon to not let Tate be in charge of the deal with Vasquez. They fought over it. Mark decided he was on a sinking ship and jumped to the other side."

Taylor shrugged. "Okay. Sucks for Jon, but why do we care about that when the cartel is coming?"

"Well," Walker said. "He's already here in St. Pete. He's a former Green Beret. And apparently Vasquez hates feds so much that he puts an extra bounty on them."

Taylor swallowed hard. "On me, you mean."

Walker nodded.

"Looks like we're in this together then," she said. "Don't worry, I'll get us plenty of help from the Bureau."

Walker shook his head. "I don't think you fully understand."

"What? Don't do that. I understand plenty. We have the might of the United States behind us."

"This is going to sound condescending no matter how I say it—"

"Then don't say it."

"I have to, Taylor. I have a very special insight into matters such as these."

"Matters such as these? What are you doing? You going to tell me you were some sort of super spy or something?" She said it with a laugh.

Walker didn't react.

Taylor gasped. "You were, weren't you?"

"I was an assassin." The words felt metallic in his mouth. Like they weren't supposed to be there.

Taylor just stared straight ahead. That sort of revelation isn't heard very often. She was speechless.

"I've been an orphan my entire life." Walker just started spilling everything. He felt comfortable with Taylor. He knew she wouldn't judge him. "I had more foster homes growing up than a business man visits hotel rooms. All but one of them were bad. The last one was the worst."

Taylor realized what Walker was saying wasn't something he shared very often. If ever. She scooted to the edge of her hospital bed and took his hand in hers. It brought Walker comfort.

"Jim used to beat all of us, but he took his miserable existence out on my foster mom, Kim, the most. I knew he was going to kill her . . ." Walker trailed off.

Taylor squeezed his hand. "It's okay. You can say it. I would never hold your past against you."

"No, but no matter what you say, you'll never look at me the same way again."

"You're right, Tom. I probably won't. But that might just be because I feel closer to you than ever."

No one called him Tom. Hearing his first name was like biting tin foil when you have a filling, it sent an electric shock all through him. But the strange thing was, that didn't feel like a bad thing coming from her mouth.

Walker said, "I knew Jim was going to kill Kim that night. I could just feel it. He was in a particularly foul mood, even for him. So . . . I beat him to it. When he started hitting her, I stopped him. I strangled him with my bare hands until he was no longer breathing."

Taylor squeezed tighter. "I'm sorry grown adults made a boy have to make such decisions. But it's not your fault. You did the right thing."

Walker went on, "Jim was connected in a 'good ole boy' kind of way with the local government. They were going to try me as an adult for his murder. And they were going to put me away."

"How old were you?"

"Fifteen."

"Dear God."

"Anyway. Long story short, and the entire reason I am telling you this, Taylor, is so you won't make the mistake of not listening to me a second time. I checked all the boxes for a black ops government program, so they snatched me from life in prison. Instead of throwing me in jail, they threw me into a life of hell. They trained me for three years. Every day. Sixteen hours a day, to become their killing machine. By the time I was twenty-five, no one was better.

"Fast forward, guys like Javier Vasquez? That's who they sent me after when all other methods of dealings failed. So, I know how he thinks. I know how guys like Mark—the Green Beret—thinks. They are like machines. Only the end goal matters. Once they've gone rogue, there is no sympathy for anyone, or anything until they get what they want."

Walker stood from his chair. "And we are what they want."

Walker watched the fear wash over Taylor. He hated to

see it, but scaring her had been his intention. Because he needed to get her attention.

"And before you say it," Walker continued. "The FBI, the CIA, and whoever else can't protect us. In fact, we need to avoid them as much as we do anyone else."

"Why?" Taylor was sitting up away from the backrest of the bed now. "I don't understand."

"Because Vasquez will get to them. I've seen it over and over again. He'll find the one who's struggling, the agent who is in debt. He'll buy them. And they'll serve us up on a platter."

"So . . ." Taylor didn't know what to say.

"I didn't come here just to visit you, or just to see if you were okay, Taylor. I came to get you out of here."

Walker could see her clutch the blanket on top of her.

"Why?" she said. "You don't think they'll . . ."

"I do. That's why we have to get out of here. Right now."

CHAPTER TWENTY-FOUR

"Do you really think all this is necessary?" Taylor said as she dressed.

Walker had his back to her. Silly, because he'd been naked with her not even a day ago, but this wasn't the time or the place.

"Maybe it isn't necessary right now, Taylor. Maybe they haven't had time to find out where you are. Or, maybe, a man who has been taught to win by being relentless has been trying to find out where you are since the minute he got off his boat last night. Because he knows I wanted to save you. So that means he might just find me too."

"Where will we go?"

"Not your place. Not mine. I've got all my stuff in my car."

"I don't have anything, Tom."

She said his name again. It wasn't easier to hear.

"Literally the clothes on my back and that's it," Taylor finished.

"We can buy more clothes."

"Okay. Fine. We can. Then what? I'm a federal agent Walker. They can't just kill me. They—"

Walker turned around as Taylor was buttoning her jeans. "That's precisely what they can do. Javier Vasquez and the Juarez Cartel have assassins too. They may not be trained like me, but that doesn't mean they aren't dangerous. And Mark, he's not an assassin, but he knows how to kill. That should be all you need to know."

"Okay fine," Taylor said as she walked over. She was in her bra, holding her t-shirt and her purse in her hand. "Then what? We get out of here, then what?"

"We survive."

Taylor frowned. "Okay. We survive. Then what?"

Walker began shaking his head. He didn't have that answer. Or, he did, but he just didn't want to say it. So he didn't. "Survive today. Then we'll worry about tomorrow."

Taylor hung her head.

"Are you okay?" Walker said. He moved over and caressed her left shoulder. Her right was heavily bandaged. "I know this is a lot. And I know you have a pretty bad concussion."

"I've been better. But I'm fine. I just . . ." Taylor looked him in the eye. "Whatever this is. Whatever I have stepped into. It's not your fight. None of it is."

"It is now."

"Why? Because Mark knows who you are?"

Walker nodded. "Yeah, that. And, they're after you. I won't let these people hurt you."

They looked at each other for a moment. Neither one of them really knew what they were to each other yet. It was clear they liked each other. It was obvious that under other circumstances, both of them would make each other a priority until it wasn't working any more. But throwing all of the trouble in on a blossoming relationship convoluted everything. They were already on fire for each other. The world burning around them would only fuel that flame. But they had to keep their heads.

Taylor leaned in first. Walker followed. They shared a long kiss. Neither of them wanted to end it. They both knew that once they did, reality was going to spoil it all. Then the door pushed open. Walker whipped around and put his hand to his concealed holster that was tucked between his lower abdomen and his jeans. Then he quickly slid his hand away when he noticed the person who'd walked in was wearing a lab coat.

"What the hell is going on?" a woman in a white lab coat said as she stopped and put her hands on her hips. She had her gray hair pulled into a ponytail with her glasses resting on top of her head. She looked young for her gray hair, but if she continued to scowl like she was at Taylor and Walker, her wrinkles would catch up with her hair soon. Taylor and Walker just stood waiting.

"You can't leave now, Ms. Crenshaw," the doctor said. "You lost a lot of blood, and your concussion is severe."

"It's a federal emergency ma'am," Taylor said. "I don't want to go, but I have to."

"The hell you do," the doctor said. "You're going to put your gown back on and get some rest. I'll tell whoever you report to that anything else just isn't an option."

Jason came barging into the room. Walker saw Taylor cover herself out of the corner of his eye.

"Shit, sorry Agent Crenshaw," he said.

"What is it, Jason?" Taylor said.

"Um, do you know anyone that maybe would try to send you flowers?"

Walker's phone buzzed in his pocket.

"Flowers?" Taylor said. "No. Why?"

Walker opened his phone as they spoke to each other.

"There's a guy in the lobby with some. He told the receptionist they're for you. She told him to leave them but he said he was told to deliver them personally."

Walker closed his phone immediately. "It's a decoy."

"What?" Taylor was flabbergasted.

Walker turned to the doctor. "Get everyone out of this hospital as fast as possible. Everyone is in danger."

The doctor's mouth slacked open. "What? I can't—"

"People are going to die if you don't," Walker said. Then he pulled his pistol from its holster for effect. It worked. The doctor backpedaled and ran out the door.

"What the hell is going on?" Jason said.

"Everyone knows that if an injured cop, or agent in this case is in the hospital, they aren't going to tell a stranger which room they're in," Walker said. "How'd you know about this?"

"I was waiting in the lobby," Jason said. "Trying to give you all some space because I looked in and you were both asleep. Heard the guy say Taylor's name so I listened in."

Walker looked over at her and took her t-shirt after he holstered his pistol. "They already know your name. We have to go. Here, I'll help you."

Taylor didn't say anything, she just gingerly raised her injured arm as high as she could. Walker slowly began putting on her shirt.

"What the hell is going on?" Jason said.

Taylor took charge. "Jason, walk the hall here, make sure there is no one who looks suspicious." She grunted in pain as she said it.

"What? Suspicious of what? What is happening?"

Walker butted in. "They'll be wearing a hat. Pulled low. No idea their nationality so don't work off of skin color. When they see you, they will react. You'll know when you see it. And when you do, take cover immediately. We aren't dealing with people who give a single shit about protocols, rules, or laws. They will shoot you."

Jason looked to Taylor. "I don't know what's happening."

"Listen to him, Jason. Please. If you don't see anyone suspicious, just come back and tell us."

Jason threw up his hands. "Whatever you say." Then he walked out shaking his head.

Walker finished helping Taylor and he threw her purse around his neck. "Sorry, I don't mean to overstep."

"Overstep. Please. I am trained, but not for this."

Walker nodded. "Stay behind me. And no matter what, don't run off. I can't protect you if I can't see you."

With that, the two of them walked toward the door. Walker could hear the rain coming down hard against the window now. But it wasn't nearly as loud as the gunshots coming from the hallway.

CHAPTER TWENTY-FIVE

As Walker approached the hospital room door, with his gun drawn, and Taylor at his back, he couldn't help but be surprised by how fast the gunmen came. And he didn't like the unfamiliar feeling of not being ready.

"Is this really happening?" Taylor said, her grip tight on the waistline of his jeans.

Walker could hear a shake in her voice. He needed to reconcile with himself that just because she was an FBI agent, it didn't mean she had an ounce of experience in an actual gunfight. He needed to regard her as a civilian, and proceed accordingly. But he didn't like hearing her short of breath.

Walker turned to her. "Look at me." She did. "I'm going to get you out of here. Understand? Just do what I say, when I say it. If you feel faint or something like that because of your injuries, you have to let me know."

She nodded, fighting back emotion. "Okay."

"You good?"

"I'll be fine. I'll stay with you."

Walker kissed her forehead. He thought about just telling

her to get in the bathroom and lock the door, but he was short on a lot of necessary information. Who these people were, where they were, and how many there were of them. For all he knew, he could take out one or two men in the hospital, only to walk into an ambush in the parking lot. Which they would most certainly be there waiting.

The gunshots had stopped, but he knew the danger was still present. He heard a loud gasp, and a faint scream from outside the door. That meant the gunman was still moving. He gave the hallway a look through the door's window, but only found walls. The nurses station was to the right, about four room-lengths down on the left. Too far away to see without opening the door.

Walker had to assume that by then, the men looking for him, and or Taylor, had already made someone give up her room information. Walker looked back over his shoulder and noticed Taylor's rolling breakfast cart. He walked over to it.

"Can you find me a mirror?" he asked her.

Taylor didn't hesitate, she immediately reached inside her purse. Walker was pushing the cart over toward the door.

"Just a small compact mirror. That work?"

Walker looked up and grabbed it as he walked by. "Perfect. Listen. This isn't like a movie. It's going to go faster than you can keep up with. I just need you to keep up with me. We can process everything once we get out of here alive.

"Okay. Blinders on. Got it."

Walker turned and grabbed her attention. "Taylor, they're not shooting anymore. That means Jason is probably dead."

Her breath caught.

"It also means they know where your room is, and they have realized that we know they are there. They will be shooting to kill."

Her lip was trembling.

"But they won't shoot you. Okay? I won't let them. Just

keep moving, no matter what you see. Just keep moving with me. We are not going to stop until we get down to the Emergency Room exit. We'll talk then. Okay?"

"O-okay."

"Blinders on."

Taylor nodded.

"Get the door for me?"

She moved around the cart and pulled open the door. Walker flipped the compact makeup mirror open. Next, he pushed the cart to the edge of the hallway wall, just out of anyone's range of sight. He looked at Taylor and nodded.

It's time.

Walker moved to the edge of the wall and positioned the mirror so he could see into the hallway. Just a flash. Just enough to get a mental picture of where everyone was standing. He learned a lot from that quick view, not the least of which was that the men were ready, because they began firing immediately. He heard Taylor squeal behind him.

"Stay with me!" he whisper-shouted to her.

Walker pushed the cart out into he hallway. It was clear the men had no trigger discipline after they fired at his mirror. Counting on that fact, he moved out into the hallway as they fired at the first thing they'd seen, the rolling cart.

The man on the right was easy, he was standing against the wall, only a waist-high gurney as a shield. Walker's two shots landed right around the man's chest. The second gunman had a lot more cover. He was standing behind the nurses station, and behind the computer on top of its desk. Walker's first round hit the computer, but it was enough to make the man flinch, and duck behind the desk. Walker made sure the hallway behind him was clear before he moved.

He did as he had told Taylor they would, and just continued his momentum forward.

"Everyone down!" Walker shouted. "Get on the ground!"

Walker figured the man would stay low and wait for him to come around the corner of the desk where the hallway opens up to the left. So, instead, he hopped up on the desk, stepped around the computer, and fired down on the man as he was pointing his gun in the wrong direction. Walker looked back and waived for Taylor to follow.

"Which way to the stairs?" Walker asked the nurse cowering behind the desk.

"Just keep going straight, they'll—they'll be on your right."

"Have you seen any more gunman?"

Her eyes were wide and he could see that her mascara streaked in her tears as she shook her head no.

Walker hopped down off the desk, took Taylor's hand, and pulled her close. His gun hand was still stretched out in front of him. Up on his right, down the hallway, he could see Jason laying lifeless up against the wall. Blood running onto the light colored tiles beneath him. Taylor involuntarily squeezed Walker's hand a little harder when she saw it, but she did as directed and just kept moving. The fire alarm began blaring. He was happy someone had been smart enough to pull the alarm to try to get people out of the building.

Walker watched every doorway as they moved for the stairs. He opened the door, gave quick look, and when he saw and heard nothing in the stairwell, he nodded for Taylor to move forward. She followed him down the stairs until they came to a door with a "2" above it. Then one more flight where they saw the number "1".

As Walker approached the door, there were no gunshots. There were no screams coming from frightened nurses or patients. It was very quiet. When Walker first entered the hospital, he did what he always does, anywhere he goes. He took mental notes of where things were. It was a product of his training. Always be aware, and always beware. His awareness taught him that this was the end of the hospital the Emergency Room entrance was on.

He knew that whoever had sent men inside the hospital, most certainly placed people outside just in case Walker and Taylor got away. He knew they'd be watching his car, but they wouldn't be watching for an ambulance. Now he just had to hope there was an ambulance conveniently sitting out front. With the storm coming in, there was a good chance they were all out picking people up.

Walker moved to the door and checked the window. In front of him he could see a waiting area full of chairs. It was empty. People had, for the most part, been evacuated after the gunshots. The fire alarm was still giving off its shrill *beep, beep, beep!* Beyond the empty chairs was the large double doors that led to the roundabout ambulance drop-off. Walker couldn't make out whether there was an ambulance there or not.

Out of the corner of his eye he saw movement. It was a man wearing a navy blue EMT jacket with a white Rod of Asclepius symbol in the middle. He was jogging toward the double doors. Probably to get away in his ambulance. This was their chance.

Walker threw open the door and tugged Taylor along. He jogged toward the Emergency Room exit as he moved his pistol to make sure no gunmen were waiting at the hospital's welcoming station. Then he checked on down the hall. There was no sign of anyone else with a gun. The EMT had not seen Walker and he jogged straight out the door. Walker followed. As he was moving through the automatic sliding door, a shiny, boxy, white and orange vehicle was there waiting.

The EMT disappeared around the back to get to the

driver's side. Walker pulled Taylor along to the back of the ambulance. He timed pulling the handle on the back door to exactly when the EMT started the engine. He held his index finger up to his lips as he ushered Taylor inside the back. Then he began crawling inside himself. Just as he was about to shut the door, he looked out at the parking lot and saw a man standing beside a black pickup truck. The man had already noticed Walker climbing in the back of the ambulance, and he rushed over to his driver's side door.

The men with the gunmen had seen Walker and Taylor getting in the ambulance.

So much for a secret getaway.

CHAPTER TWENTY-SIX

The palm trees in Jon's backyard were bending so much from the wind that it looked as though they might just pull right up out of the ground. The usually calm intracoastal waterway was all white caps, the water in his pool the same. He'd been staring out the back window for at least five minutes. His phone was in his hand. Waiting. He'd messaged Walker to see if he and his friend were okay and hadn't heard anything back. In the short amount of time he'd stood there, the storm had doubled in ferocity.

His doorbell rang. Reflex had him grab his Glock that was sitting on the table beside him. His video doorbell app notification popped up on his phone. He tapped it and the video from his doorbell came into view. His son Tate was standing there looking like a wet dog. Jon's stomach dropped. He didn't have the time, or the energy to deal with Tate right now.

The doorbell rang again. In the video on his phone he watched Tate duck down and speak into the camera. "Come on dad. I know you see me."

The next thought that flashed in Jon's mind scared him. *What if Mark had followed Tate?*

It would be icing on the proverbial cake if his son did him in once and for all. Neither shocking, or surprising. Either way, Jon was going to have to let him in if for nothing else than to tell him to get lost. To Miami. Today. And don't look back. Jon crossed the living room and into the foyer. Jon opened the oversized front door. Tate just stood there on the front porch, soaking wet, staring at him. Driving rain was blowing across the street behind him.

"Why the hell are you just standing there?" Jon said.

Tate didn't speak. Instead, his eyes twitched to his left. Jon knew immediately that Mark was out there with him.

"Put the gun down, Jon." Mark said. He had to raise his voice over the whipping wind.

"He said he'd kill me if I didn't lead him here," Tate said.

A lot of scenarios played in fast forward through Jon's mind. The highlights were that he could step out and try to shoot Mark, but even though Jon was good with a gun, Mark was better. He also could make a run for the garage, hop into his Bronco and blast through the garage door, then drive as fast as he could to get out of there. But ultimately what he'd settled on without knowing it was taking a shot at tugging at Mark's heartstrings—if he had any heartstrings at all.

"What are we doing here, Mark?" Jon said. "I thought we were a team?"

"We were a team, Jon. But teammates listen to each other. It's how a team wins. You not listening to me about Tate here made us lose. I don't like to be a part of a losing team."

"So you found a new team? A drug cartel? That's not you Mark, you're better than that."

Jon stepped out onto the front porch, still holding his gun

down by his side. Mark was leaning back against the white stucco rail on Jon's right.

"I told you to put the gun down, Jon. See? You don't listen."

Jon could see that Mark wasn't holding a gun. He had balls. Jon knew he also covered all angles.

"Where's Terry?" Jon said. Terry was Mark's sniper friend that he'd brought along as security on a lot of Jon's jobs.

"Don't worry about Terry, Jon."

"What the hell do you want then, Mark? You bring Tate here? Why? You have me now, so let him go? What do you— what does Vasquez want from me?"

"From you?" Mark stood from his leaning position. "Penance for your transgressions."

"He doesn't want me to sell his drugs for him anymore?"

Mark shook his head. "No. He realized, after last night, that it is beyond your capabilities."

"So, what then?"

"All your weapons. The entire stock."

A small price to pay in Jon's mind. He owed Vasquez twenty million. He probably only had seven million in weapons. Jon couldn't help but feel a little hopeful that he might actually get out of this damn nightmare.

"Okay," Jon said. "No problem. Take them."

"We already are. Got a truck full of men in Miami loading them up now."

"Fine. That it?" Thunder crackled overhead. Tate jumped a little at the sound of it. "And you'll leave Tom Walker and his friend alone now too?"

Mark nodded. "You know . . . I would, but . . . Vasquez already sent some men after them at the hospital. That problem is already taken care of. You see, you should have had me taking care of a lot more things than just being your muscle, Jon."

Jon's heart sank. Walker was a good man. He couldn't believe that all of this mess he had created—that Tate had created—had cost innocent people their lives. He felt sick.

"You're a real asshole, Mark."

"Guess being an asshole is only okay if I'm working for you."

"So go on then," Jon said. "Sounds like you've got what you want. What Vasquez wants. So just leave us the hell alone."

Mark shook his head and made a tsk tsk sound. "Once again Jon, you don't listen."

"What the hell are you talking about now?"

"Penance, Jon. Remember? Vasquez won't let his losses go unpunished."

"You're taking everything my business has, Mark. That's not enough?"

"It's not enough."

Mark's tone was cold. Jon was trying to decide if Mark had ever really been the team player he'd thought he was, or had he always just been waiting for something better to come along?

"What then, Mark? Huh? What the fuck else?"

"Now you don't have to lose your temper, Jon. This is no one's fault but your own."

"Yeah, I've heard that speech already. Tell me what you want or get the hell off my property."

Mark nodded toward Tate. "Shoot him."

Jon laughed. "I don't have time for this, Mark. You need to go."

"Shoot him and I'll go. Your debt to Vasquez will be settled."

"I'm not going to shoot my son. But I will shoot you if you don't leave now."

"This is all Tate's fault, Jon," Mark said. "You know it. I know it. And Vasquez knows it."

Jon raised his gun, pointing it directly at Mark's chest. "I'm not going to ask you again. Get off my property."

Mark didn't protest. He didn't even raise his hands. He simply uttered two words that would haunt Jon for the rest of his life. "Do it."

When the right side of Tate's face disappeared into a pink mist, it was as if Jon was seeing things. Even though he felt his son's blood and brains smack against him, he stood emotionless as Tate's body collapsed in a heap onto the ground. It couldn't be real. Things like this don't actually happen. Jon just wanted the nightmare to end. He just wanted to wake up.

He thought he heard someone's voice, but it sounded distant. Like it was coming from a block away. He wasn't waking up. And his son's body, lying bleeding out at his feet, was real.

"Put the gun down Jon or I'm going to have Terry shoot you too!"

Before Jon could register what Mark was shouting, the gun slipped from his hand. He had no control over his body at the moment. He was in shock. But he had to snap out of it.

Snap out of it!

Mark lunged for Jon's gun. Reality came whipping back through Jon's consciousness. His body—almost absent of his mind—realized that if he didn't move that he was going to die too.

Jon squatted to pick up his gun but he was too slow. Mark was already on him. He drove Jon back inside the house and planted him on his back. They both slid across the hardwood floor. Jon was able to use Mark's momentum to flip him over, but before Jon could get all the way back to the door, Mark grabbed his foot and pulled him down. He reached for his gun that lay just beyond the threshold, right in front of his dead son, but he came up just short.

"Stop fighting me, Jon!" Mark shouted as he pulled himself on top of Jon.

Jon felt reality slipping. "You killed my son!"

Mark shook his head. "*You* killed your son!"

With a jolt of adrenaline Jon bucked his hips and Mark went flying off of him. But he went flying toward the door. Right beside Jon's gun. Jon watched Mark look over at it. Jon looked back toward the back of his house. Outside the weather was terrible, but his boat docked right out in the back yard might be his only way out. No matter how choppy the water might be. He just needed enough time to get there.

Mark moved toward the gun and Jon did the only thing he could think of. He swung his legs around and kicked at Mark's back before Mark could fully get his balance. As Mark was toppling over, Jon jumped up and lunged for the front door. Just before he slammed it he saw Mark raising the gun, then he disappeared. Jon dead-bolted the door just as Mark fired the gun. Jon took off running for the back door.

Jon heard Mark's muffled shout. "There's nowhere to run, Jon!"

But he was running anyway. He threw open the back door and sprinted by the pool. Before the chaos began with Mark, Jon had been tending to the boat to make sure it was secure in the weather so he had the keys in his pocket. Something that just might save his life. *If* he had time to get the lift down and the boat in the water.

Jon almost slipped when he hit the wood-planked boat ramp, but he grabbed a pole and righted himself just before he went down. He glanced back over his shoulder and didn't see anyone coming. He pushed the down button on the mechanical boat lift and all the sudden he was stuck in slow motion.

He glanced back at the house again. Still nothing. Rain was pelting him in the face. The wind was blowing so hard he had to squint just to keep his eyes open enough to see what he was doing. The boat was lowering, but it was taking forever. Like, two seconds per inch kind of slow, and he was out in the open without a weapon. He could feel the anxiety building. There was at least another foot to go before the boat could be moved.

Jon saw movement at the right side of the house. He ducked down, getting low behind a metal storage bin screwed down to the dock. The boat lift sounded loud to him, but over the wind and the rain, there was no way they could hear it from the house. Could they? Jon's anxiety was at full tilt. He'd just seen his son gunned down right in front of him. According to Mark, the only man left in the world who could help Jon had just been hunted down and killed at the hospital. And now, a Green Beret was hunting him. He felt as if his heart might explode.

Jon took a deep breath and peeked up over the top of the bin. He immediately lost every single bit of that air because he'd just been spotted.

Mark was coming right for him.

CHAPTER TWENTY-SEVEN

When Walker slammed the back door of the ambulance shut, the EMT behind the wheel turned around in horror. Walker was surprised to see an opening from the driver's seat into the back of the ambulance, but he had never been in one so what did he know? Walker had to move quick because the gunmen had just watched him and Taylor climb inside from across the parking lot. And they had already moved inside their truck to give chase. Thankfully, Taylor's brain wasn't too concussed, and she thought to pull her FBI credentials and flashed them to the EMT.

"FBI! Drive! Drive! Drive!"

Walker didn't know if he would have had the EMT drive or not. He didn't want to endanger another innocent bystander, but it didn't really matter. The EMT nodded, threw the ambulance into drive, and floored the gas. Walker fell back on his ass, but was able to keep Taylor upright on the bench.

"What are we working with here?" the EMT said.

Walker was taken aback by the question. Not only did the driver not seem shaken by the fact that he had to drive away from active shooters, but he had an astonishingly calm demeanor when he asked what they were working with.

The EMT beat Walker to the question, "I'm a Marine! Three tours in Iraq, now tell me what I need to know!"

Walker snapped to it when he heard the word Marine. "I'm not from here, but we need to get to St. Pete Beach. Near Caddy's on the beach. You know it?"

"I know it. Who the hell are these guys?"

Walker moved around the gurney. "You okay?" he said to Taylor. She nodded. He went on up to the passenger seat. The EMT had just flipped on the emergency lights and siren, and Walker had to hold on as he made a sharp right. He saw Taylor fastening her seatbelt behind him. He then pulled his pistol and ejected the magazine to see how many rounds he had left. Seven.

"I'm Walker. These guys are cartel, and they want us dead. You do not have to be apart of this."

"Looks like I do now, so lets leave that shit for later. I'm Jax. I'm not supposed to be carrying, but I'm strapped. No way I'd do this job without a piece with how many crazy assholes are running around these days."

Jax lifted his coat and revealed a gun in a concealed holster tucked in the front of his pants. The black pistol was only a couple of shades darker than Jax's skin. Now that Walker was closer he could see the Marine in him. Thick neck, thick thighs, and whether it was because of habit or not, he also kept his hair buzzed. He couldn't have been much older than thirty.

Walker checked the side mirror, he didn't see anyone racing toward them yet. "Well, your bad luck in finding yourself in this situation is apparently my good luck. Thanks for driving."

"You military too?" Jax said.

"Black ops." It was just easier to say that than to try to

explain that he never officially served in any formal capacity. And, it was the truth.

"Some real shit, huh? Intel or field?"

"They only called me when it was time for the enemy to die."

"My man," Jax said.

"You ever used that thing?" Walker nodded toward Jax's midsection.

"You asking me if I've killed someone? Isn't that a faux pas or something?"

"Kind of relevant right now though, isn't it?" Walker said, "seeing as how we have gunmen trying to run us down."

Jax looked over and gave a half smile. "I like you. No bullshit. Yeah, I've used it."

"I can tell. This doesn't seem to be phasing you too much."

"You either," Jax said. "I've been in a few hairy situations." He jerked his head over to the side mirror. "We've got company."

"You just worry about driving. I'll worry about these guys."

"About ten minutes to Caddy's, maybe fifteen with the weather. That really where you're trying to go?"

"No, but get me there I'll get us the rest of the way."

"You got it."

Jax swerved around some cars waiting at a red light. Walker moved passed Taylor who was holding on for dear life. Through the back window Walker could see the black pickup truck swerving in and out of traffic. They weren't going to get out of this without more bullets.

Walker looked back at Taylor. "You good?"

"No, but I'm fine. I have my pistol in my purse. Jason stuck it in there when they were wheeling me in last night."

Walker nodded. "We might need it."

Taylor hung her head.

"I'm sorry about Jason."

"Me too," she said without looking up. She was holding on to the back of the bench seat with both arms. "Thank you, Tom."

"No reason to thank me. I haven't gotten you out of this yet."

"Doesn't matter. The only reason I'm alive right now is because you came for me. You could be halfway to Europe right now. But you came back for me."

Walker looked over. She was looking at him.

"Thank you," she finished.

Walker nodded. He didn't know what else to say. He quite possibly would walk through fire for her, but it didn't need to be said.

"How we doing, Jax?"

"Luckily the rain has let up a little. But there are still way too many people on the road for this weather."

Walker thought of the message he'd received just before shit hit the fan at the hospital. It had been from Jon. He was messaging to check in on him. Walker pulled out his phone and tapped on Jon's number. It rang several times then went to voicemail. He couldn't help but think the worst.

Jax swerved again. Walker looked behind them. The truck was getting closer. There was no way they were going to make it all the way to Jon's house without having to deal with them.

Taylor caught his eye. "They're going to catch us, aren't they."

He wanted to lie to her. It would have been easier. But taking the easy way up front only makes everything harder later. "They are. But I'll be ready. We just have to hang on tight if they try to run us off the road."

Taylor nodded. If she was scared, she wasn't letting on.

Jax had been a Godsend. But Walker didn't know if it would be enough. If *he* could be enough to stop these guys with only seven bullets. He glanced back out the window. They were definitely getting closer. It was almost time to find out if he could make it happen or not.

CHAPTER TWENTY-EIGHT

Mark was coming for him. Jon didn't have a choice but to jump on the boat and fire it up. It wasn't quite in the water yet, but it was close. If the propellers could just catch enough water he might be able to reverse the boat off the lift. If not, he's dead. Either way, he couldn't wait any longer.

Jon rose up and jumped over into the boat. Mark must have been running with his gun drawn because two bullets smacked into the top front of the boat. Jon crawled forward, madly trying to reach the steering column. He pushed the key into the ignition and turned it. As soon as the engine started he pulled the throttle back as he held the trim button down, trying his best to get the outboard motor down into the water as fast as he could.

The engine roared but there was no gurgle of water, and no movement of the boat. Jon knew it was taking too long. Mark was going to catch him. As a last ditch effort, he grabbed a water ski that was laying on the deck off to his left. When he rose up, Mark was leaping off of the dock. Jon swung the ski as hard as he could and hit Mark right in the chest, sending him crashing onto the rail of the boat. His legs were inside the boat, but he was on his back, with his torso hanging out over the edge.

Jon could have pushed him off, but the impact with Mark sent Jon flying to the deck on the opposite side of the boat. He scrambled to his feet as Mark pulled himself up. Jon went to run at him, but his foot slipped, and he hit the deck. When Mark raised up, he'd managed to keep his gun in his hand. Jon knew it was over. He stared right at Mark. He at least wanted to make the traitor look him in the eyes while he shot him.

That's when the propellers caught water and the boat went flying backward off the boat lift. The force was too great for Mark to maintain his balance and before he could pull the trigger he went toppling backward off the boat. By the grace of God, Jon had survived.

Then he remembered how close the other side of the inlet was to his boat dock. He jumped to his feet and dove for the throttle. He punched the stick with his fist and the boat jerked forward so hard that it slammed him into the captain's chair. He reached up and pulled the boat into neutral. When he looked back over the stern, he was only a couple of feet from the concrete on that side.

The boat was wobbling wildly back and forth in the raging tropical storm waters. He looked over the bow and saw Mark battling the waves. Jon was just about to go and run him over, but then he remembered Terry.

The sniper.

Jon forced the throttle forward and just as he did a round went through the seat cushion of the captains chair beside him. He turned the wheel to send the boat in the direction of the waterway and then dropped to the deck. He heard another thump from another bullet somewhere behind him. He stayed down as long as he could, but he was going to have to raise up and steer. The waves were throwing the boat everywhere, and in the middle of the waterway were wooden posts anchored into the floor of the ocean. If he hit one of those, it would be as bad as taking a sniper round to the neck.

He managed to move over to the throttle and pull it back to neutral. He didn't know if Terry could hit him from where Jon was in the water now or not, but he wanted to make it as hard for him to be hit as possible. He poked his head up, then right back down. Luckily, he was close to the middle of the waterway. From the deck, he reached up and turned the wheel a little more to the right, then pushed the throttle forward again.

Jon used this method for the next couple of minutes, until he was sure he was out of range. The rain had picked back up again. He was as wet as he would have been if he were in the ocean itself. The wheel had a canvas covering over top of it so it helped shield him a little from the rain. He sat back down and steered the boat away from his home, and away from his son who he would never see, or speak to again.

Just as a lightning bolt flashed off in the distance, he noticed his phone was lying on the deck by his foot. When he picked it up he saw that he had two missed calls. From Tom Walker. As the waves threw him left and right he opened his phone to see what time the calls were from, but he knew they couldn't have been long ago.

The last missed call was just a minute ago. That son of a bitch had made it out of the hospital alive!

Jon pressed the contact number and the phone began to ring.

"Jon!" Walker answered. "You have to get out of that house!"

"Yeah. I figured that out the hard way!" Jon had to shout

over all the noise from the weather and the boat. "How'd you make it out of the hospital?"

"Carefully. How'd you know?"

"Just had a run in with Mark. Don't know how I survived, but my son didn't! He's dead, Walker! That son of a bitch killed him!"

Walker's end of the line was quiet.

"Where are you now?" Jon said. "I'm on my boat heading South!"

"I'm sorry, Jon. Sorry about your son. But what the hell are you doing in the water in this weather?"

"Only choice I had!" A big wave nearly tossed Jon's boat into the marker pole. He had to steer it back to the right of middle. "You getting the hell out of town?"

"I wish. I've got a tail, Jon. Trying figure out—"

It was hard for Jon to hear anything, but Walker cut out abruptly, and it sounded like screeching tires and the click clack of a dropped phone.

"Walker!"

He didn't hear anything. The rain was coming down even harder. Slapping his right arm as the wind drove it in from the West.

"Walker!"

Jon heard some rustling. "Jon, I gotta go. We're in trouble. The gunmen called ahead and had some more of their men cut us off on the drawbridge."

"Drawbridge?" Jon shouted. "You mean Corey Causeway? But that's a divided four lane bridge!"

"Yeah, and they drove down the wrong way to cut us off. Bye Jon. Good luck."

"Wait! Walker!"

"I have to go, Jon!"

"I'm close! In the water! It's not a big drop, you can jump and we can get out of here!"

"How long?" Walker said, sounding hopeful.

"Two minutes, tops!"

"I'll try to hold them off!"

The call ended.

Jon pushed the throttle even harder. He didn't care how bumpy the ride was. The prospect of helping someone have a chance to live after watching his son die gave him purpose. And it was the only feeling keeping him going at that moment.

He could see the Corey Causeway up ahead through the torrential downpour, and the whitecap waves. He was going to make. He had to.

CHAPTER TWENTY-NINE

Walker pocketed his phone and gripped his pistol. Jon had called just when Walker was about out of ideas on how to get Taylor out of there safely. Now he just had to keep these men at bay long enough to get to Jon's boat.

"What are we going to do, boss?" Jax said from the front of the ambulance. "They could start shooting any second."

Walker had moved to the back when the three vehicles blocked their path to get off of the bridge. The black pickup truck that had been following them was joined by silver SUV. They were blocked in on both sides. Taylor wasn't reacting to anything that was going on. Walker could see that she was just trying to keep herself calm.

"You're supposed to be able to get out of this kind of stuff, right?" Jax spoke again.

"Can this ambulance plow through those trucks in front of us?" Walker said.

"If we would have had the chance to get a lot more speed? Sure. But those are some big vehicles blocking us. Might make it. But if we don't, we're all three dead."

Walker thought the same thing. Their safest out was the

boat. Walker moved to the front and looked out the passenger window. Through the storm he could see a lone boat coming their way.

"It's Jon!" Walker said. "Time to get out of here!"

Taylor looked up with hope in her eyes.

"Jax, you're going to put the back of the ambulance to the rail. We'll go out through there. That should give us cover enough to jump. As soon as we hit the water, get in the boat. Then we ride out of here. Got it?"

Jax nodded as he put the ambulance in reverse. Walker looked back at Taylor. She nodded as well.

"Listen to me, now," Walker said. "There can be zero hesitation when we get to the rail. They will be shooting. Understand?"

He looked at Jax for confirmation, then Taylor. They both nodded. "No hesitation." He walked to the back and opened the door.

The men began shooting. Bullets pounded against the ambulance. Taylor let out a yelp as she stood.

"Let's go!" Walker said as he took Taylor's hand.

Jax moved the ambulance's back end to the rail. Walker was holding the door open until it was pinned open by the rail. Rain was bouncing off the rail and the floor of the ambulance.

"Jax, you first! You can help Taylor up out of the water and onto the boat."

Jax came walking back. Walker caught him by the shoulders. "Thank you, Jax."

Jax nodded. Walker reached down the front of Jax's pants and took his pistol.

"What are you doing?" Taylor said.

"I'm just going to hold them off while the two of you jump. Come on! Let's go!"

Gunfire continued around them and the sound of bullets

hitting the ambulance was maddening.

Jax looked Walker in the eyes. There was a smirk on his face. He knew Walker's plan. "Good luck, Walker. I'll make sure she's safe."

Walker nodded.

"What? What does he mean?" Taylor said.

Jax moved to the back, put his foot on the rail, then pushed himself out and away from the bridge. He was gone.

"The water is going to be really choppy," he said to Taylor. "Make sure you get a good breath now, and don't panic when it takes them a second to pull you up into the boat, okay?" He moved her to the back, the rail was right in front of them.

"You mean when you help me onto the boat, right?"

Walker leaned in and kissed her on the forehead.

"Walker?"

Walker picked her up and tossed her over the side. "Deep breath!"

"Walker!" she shouted as she disappeared from sight.

Walker looked out over the rail, he could see Jon circling to get to them. He leaned out around the back of the ambulance and fired a couple of shots left, and a couple to the right. A feeble attempt to keep them from moving to the side of the bridge and shoot down, but he had to do something. The bigger something was getting their attention by plowing right through the two trucks behind him. He couldn't risk it not working when Jax and Taylor were inside. Now that he was alone, he only had to worry about himself. And that was his comfort zone in a life and death situation.

Walker rushed to the front and plopped down into the driver's seat. The driver's seat window was already missing. Walker had sat right in the glass, but his jeans were enough to keep it from cutting him. He put the ambulance in drive, turned toward the black pickup truck and the silver SUV, and floored the gas peddle. He ducked down behind the wheel to avoid the couple of bullets that made it through the windshield. He pushed his body forward, up against the wheel so the slam he would take when the ambulance hit the vehicles would be minimized.

Walker kept his foot on the gas as he leaned forward. Then came the crash. His head got tossed against the top of the steering wheel and purple stars burst in front of his eyes. The ambulance only slowed for a second, then it broke free from the vehicles and sped forward. Walker sat up and looked out over the hood, that's when he side swiped another car that had yet to turn around from the bridge being blocked, then he had to swerve over to his right to avoid another car. This put him on the side of the road with the proper flow of traffic, which, luckily, was very sparse at the moment.

Walker tried to check the side mirror, but it was gone. He turned and looked over his right shoulder, out the open back door, and saw that the three vehicles from the other side of the bridge were just driving through the two he had plowed. They were going to catch him, and it wasn't going to take them very long. He needed a next step, and he needed it fast.

He couldn't help but second guess his decision to not jump to the boat below. He knew they were going to get some place safe. Walker also knew that Mark would not stop coming for them. Military men like Mark can't stand it if a job goes unfinished. Walker felt like Vasquez had a lot bigger fish to fry, and would quickly lose interest in finding them. He'd killed Tate. Walker thought that would be enough.

Not for Mark. Mark would keep coming. Walker knew that if he could take out Mark, Vasquez would lose interest even faster. That's why he stayed in the ambulance. To put what he thought would be an end to this mess. And he could just feel it that Mark was in one of those vehicles behind him, trying to run him down.

It was time to pull himself out of the fire. And he knew the only way to do that was with fire of his own.

CHAPTER THIRTY

Walker scanned both sides of the road for a place he could lose the ambulance, and gain a tactical advantage. There weren't a lot of people out now because of the storm, but he was still trying to find a place that wouldn't have too many patrons. Up on his left, he could see a steeple. It wasn't Sunday, so he figured there wouldn't be a crowd. It was his best shot because the vehicles chasing him had already caught up to him. If he waited too long and let them turn the ambulance over, he was a dead man.

Walker glanced back over his shoulder and sure enough, there was a white pickup truck directly behind him. Walker turned the ambulance a little to the right, then hit the brakes, swerved left, and cut across traffic to make it into the church parking lot. Walker slammed the ambulance in park, then ran and jumped out the back immediately as the white pickup was approaching. He raised his gun and fired the last three rounds in his Sig Sauer at the driver's side of the oncoming truck's windshield.

The pickup swerved at the last second. Walker had hit him. The truck plowed forward and ran into the right side of the red brick church, banging to a stop. Walker dropped his gun and pulled Jax's pistol. It was also a Sig, albeit a different model, but it felt good in his hand. He raced around the passenger side of the truck. When he threw open the door, the dazed man inside was bleeding from the head. Walker put him out of his misery with a single bullet, then took the pistol from the man's hand.

All of the men Walker had seen coming after him thus far were Hispanic. Mark must have called in Vasquez's men to help. Luckily, they weren't used to the level of skill Walker possessed. Mark wouldn't be either, but Walker would have to be much more careful when he came around.

The backseat of the pickup was empty. Walker raced around the back and up the stairs to the church. Two SUV's were sliding sideways into the parking lot. Walker rushed through the church entrance and shut the door behind him. An older woman wearing a conservative white blouse and long maroon skirt dropped the vase she was holding. It shattered on the hardwood floor.

"Is there a back door?" Walker said.

The woman was staring at the gun in his hand. She was holding up her hands.

"I'm not going to hurt you, but I need to know if there's a back door."

The woman nodded.

"Is there anyone else here?" Walker said.

The woman shook her head.

"Get out the back door now. Go straight to your car. There are gunmen coming here right now and they will shoot you. GO!"

The woman yelped, but then took off running. Walker scanned the area. There were restrooms to the right and left of the front entrance. Just one double door leading into the chapel where the woman had just fled. There was an aisle left, right, and middle of all the pews, a stage at the far end of the room that held the podium, and the risers for the choir were behind it. To the right of the stage was the door the woman ran through. Walker didn't see daylight when she opened it so there might be more to the building on the other side.

Walker moved into the chapel and shut the double doors behind him. He ran down the middle aisle and over to the back door. He opened it, and just like the front, there were restrooms and an exit to the outside. He couldn't watch both entrances, so he needed help. On the wall to his left, there was a table holding a dozen or more handbells. *Perfect*.

Walker opened a door that was on his right, it was a janitor's closet. He grabbed the mop and moved toward the double door back exit. He slid the mop handle through the handles on each of the doors. The goal wasn't to keep them out, it was to force them to break the door in. This would knock over the table of handbells that he was currently placing in front of the doors. He would at least hear them enter.

He hurried back into the chapel. He decided it was best to go about halfway into the room and duck behind a pew. Walker didn't know what guns the men would have, but any of the rounds they held would make it through one pew. But several rows on both his front and back would be good protection. He had eleven rounds left in Jax's gun, and a full twelve round magazine in the one he took off the dead man in the pickup. He knew those twenty-three bullets were going to be gone in a blink. That was his only real worry.

The front doors crashed inward. Walker took a knee at the edge of the pew and peered down the middle aisle toward the chapel's entrance. His gun at the ready. The men who were coming for him were going to have to open the door to get to him. They wouldn't survive not knowing where Walker was on the other side. He would give them no time to search.

The handle rattled on the chapel doors. Walker took aim. He was quite cold from bringing his rain-soaked body inside the air-conditioned church, but other than that his aim was steady. The door cracked slightly. There were no other noises in the building so every inch the door opened, the creak echoed in the open space. Walker waited patiently.

Finally, the nose of a rifle slipped though the crack. The man holding it tried to run for the first row of pews, but there was too much space. Walker fired three times. He watched two of them hit the man. The next guy in line had the nose of his rifle poking out the doorway, but when he saw his amigo drop to the ground, he pulled it back.

Walker one, cartel gunmen zero.

He stayed patient, holding his position. He liked where he was in the building. As long as he had ammo, he was going to be okay.

Behind him came a crash of handbells. His cover situation just doubled in complication. Now he would have to watch his front, and his back. Vastly more difficult, but he had no where else to go, and zero other options available to him.

So far he still liked his odds. But he didn't know exactly how long that was going to last. It all depended on how many men Vasquez sent. Walker knew very little about the Juarez Cartel. Except, of course, for its ruthless reputation. And how large it was as a whole. So, Walker could be about finished with who Vasquez sent, or this could just be the first wave of his new nightmare.

One at a time. It was the only way he could think. It was the only way forward.

CHAPTER THIRTY-ONE

EVERY MINUTE JON, TAYLOR, AND JAX WERE ON THE BOAT, the weather seemed to get progressively worse, and the waves grew substantially higher. Jon had a small tarp tucked in the storage beneath his seat. He gave it to Taylor and Jax, but the boat was bucking so wildly that it was almost impossible to shield any of the rain at all. But there was no way that Jon was going to stop that boat. Not yet. They were too close to where everything went down behind them. He didn't want to take any chances.

The problem was that he couldn't take the boat out into the Gulf of Mexico either. Without any land protection, the waves were probably twice as high there. But between Taylor begging him to turn back for Walker, and Jax vomiting everywhere, his stress level was through the roof. He knew they couldn't help Walker. They would one hundred percent get themselves killed. He tried to explain to Taylor that going back for Walker would be the last thing Walker would want them to do. But she wouldn't let it die. Now she was trying to stay in her seat, cover with a tarp, and do something on her phone.

Jax stumbled up to him in the captain's seat. He was wiping vomit from his mouth with his sleeve. "You sure this is just a tropical storm and there's not a hurricane coming?"

"I'm not sure of anything!"

Both of them were shouting over the noise of the boat and the storm.

"What are we gonna do?"

Jon just motioned for Jax to sit back down. His questions weren't helping. Especially when Jon had zero answers. He thought of his friend, Bud, in Tampa. First it somehow occurred to him that it could be his friend that turned on him and let the FBI know about the drop. But he knew better. Bud was a real one. They'd been to war together and once you forge that bond, it's unbreakable. He couldn't know how the connection was broken and given to Taylor and the FBI, that was something he'd have to ask her when this thing was over. Which, hopefully, because he was able to save her, might win some favor with her at the end of the day.

The good reminder that the thought about Bud did bring was Tampa. He could take the entire route to Tampa without ever getting out in open water. The bay would still be awful weather, but if he stayed close to the shoreline, maybe it wouldn't be so bad. And they could put some distance between them and Mark, and, or the cartel. Whoever it was that was really after them.

Taylor came rushing up to him. "I can't hear my phone! I can't even get it to work! The water must have damaged it! Can I use your phone? Please!"

"Your phone?" Jon shouted. "Really? Right now? You want my phone?"

"I'm trying to get a team to track Walker's phone so they can get to him to help since we're stuck out here in this monsoon! Please, if you have his number in your phone I can call it in and they can track it!"

That was actually a brilliant idea that Jon hadn't even thought of. "Yes! Right here!" He reached in his pocket and handed it to her.

"Is there somewhere else I can go? Taylor shouted. "I'm afraid they won't be able to hear me over this noise!"

Jon moved Taylor back a bit then reached across to undo the latch to the bathroom. "You'll have to be careful! This boat's going to toss you around, and there is nothing soft in there!"

Taylor nodded then stepped down into the bathroom. He watched as she got tossed into the sink, slipped, and fell down on her ass.

"You okay?" Jon shouted.

Taylor's sour facial expression said that she wasn't okay, but she gave a half-hearted thumbs up anyway. He watched as she sat down on top of the toilet and brought the phone to her ear as she grabbed onto the sink for dear life. He then looked over at Jax, he was lying motionless under the tarp. It was a mess, but they were alive.

Jon changed course to head for Tampa. He steered left when he got the chance and navigated the shallow waters of the intracoastal to the best of his abilities in the crazy wind that was tossing them all around. He hated to think that Walker was fighting his battle for him. Jon was having major regrets about not staying and fighting Mark at the house. But he knew that even on the one percent chance he could have beaten Mark, Vasquez would have never stopped coming for him. When you cross a man with no morals, you have to suffer the consequences. And that's why he wished he could trade places with Walker so no one had to suffer Jon's mistakes but himself.

There was nothing he could do.

Nothing but keep someone safe that Walker cared about, and hope to God that Walker could make it back to her.

That's all he had. And he owed that much to Walker at the very least.

Taylor ducked her head and crawled out of the bathroom. Jon caught her under the arm just as she was about to fall. He could see blood on the shoulder of her white shirt.

"You okay?" Jon said. "You're bleeding!"

Taylor looked at her shoulder. "Yeah. I'm okay. Souvenir from the two men you had with you last night. Thanks by the way."

Jon looked at her and he couldn't believe that she had a smile on her face. She was a tough one. "No wonder Walker likes you. And I am sorry."

"Just get me off this boat safely and we'll call it even!"

Jon saluted. "Yes ma'am."

"My team found Walker's phone! They're sending people there now. Hopefully it's not too late!"

Jon held up his hand, then he crossed his fingers.

Taylor nodded. "If you let me know where you plan on docking, I'll have some people pick us up. Make sure we have a smooth ride. I promise I won't let them know who you are. I owe you that much!"

Jon smiled. "The Pointe Marina at Harbour Island! Used to take my wife there back in the day!"

Taylor smiled and squeezed Jon's arm. She held up the phone. "Mind if I hang onto this for a few minutes?"

Jon shook his head. Then he watched her stumble back to the seat. She was checking on Jax. They both sat up and covered with the tarp. Jon navigated ahead. It wasn't going to be a fun hour, but he was going to get them safely to Tampa, even if it was the last thing he did.

CHAPTER THIRTY-TWO

Walker's head was on a swivel. Back toward the door behind him, then back to the front. Over and over again, watching for one of the men to make a mistake. He was doing his best to listen for them too, but the storm was raging outside. Thunder every few seconds, wind and rain beating against the large stained-glass windows. Impossible.

He caught the back door opening out of his right eye and he whipped his gun in that direction. The door to the back exit was not as thick as the others. Walker decided to shoot first. Two bangs and the man dropped to a knee, the door the man was standing behind flung open. Walker shot the man on his knee somewhere around his neck, but couldn't get the next shot off before a string of bullets came his way from the man standing in the now open doorway.

Walker dropped onto his right side, held the gun out—resting it on the floor—and shot twice at the gunman's feet. One round hit him and he let out a shout. Walker raised up and shot twice, putting him down. He wheeled around immediately and shot the next man trying to get the jump on him from the front door. That left him with only two rounds in Jax's gun.

Walker made the quick decision that more people would probably be out front, so he sprinted for the back door. He just needed to get to one of the men he'd killed to get to their weapon. But as he made it to the first gunman, another man was running toward him from the exit room. Walker dove for him as he raised his weapon and both of them slammed against the concrete wall at the back.

The gunman had taken the brunt of it because it was Walker driving him back into the wall. His head hit first so he was unconscious. Walker raised up on top of him and fired the last two rounds in Jax's gun. Then dropped it to the floor. The now dead man had an AR pistol strapped around his neck that Walker commandeered, along with the Glock he was carrying as his side piece. Walker was set on weapons, now the other guys were in trouble.

Until they weren't.

The back wall that Walker had just rammed the gunman into blasted into a thousand pieces. Walker felt a flash of heat as he was thrown backward—the blast so strong that it threw him all the way into the chapel. He tried to move, but he couldn't. His eyes were burning and his ears were ringing. He tried to take a breath but nothing came. It was as if he were trapped inside someone elses body and his mind couldn't move it.

It was only seconds, but to him, as he struggled to move, it felt like hours. The position he was stuck in forced him to look in one direction. The middle of the back wall of the church, just above the choir risers. An oversized Jesus was hanging from a cross. Walker had never been a religious man. It was hard to believe in God when you grow up with God's creations beating the shit out of you every other night.

That's why he never noticed that when Jesus was hanging from the cross, he looked . . . sad.

But of course he was sad. He had to be disappointed in his people. The very people he'd come to save were crucifying him. It was the first time in Walker's life that he felt like he had something in common with Jesus. It was a fleeting thought. But one that would stick with him for as long as he lived. And if he didn't get moving, he knew that wouldn't be very long.

Walker tried again for a breath, this time it came. He went to sit up and it felt like a weight was on his chest. Walker blinked heavily, then turned his head. There he saw why it felt like he was being weighted down. It was because there was a boot pressing down on his chest, and it was connected to whom he could only assume was Jon's Green Beret . . . Mark. The next thing Walker saw was the muzzle of a gun. Beyond that, Mark's dark brown gotee morphed into a smile.

Finally, the world came back to Walker's ears in a whoosh, and he could hear again.

"I expected more after you talked such a big game out on that boat. I'm a little disappointed you were so easy. Now tell me . . . where's Jon?"

Walker wouldn't have been able to talk even if he wanted too. It was hard enough to get air in his lungs in order to breathe.

"I will not ask you again," Mark said. "And if I have to shoot you before you tell me where he is, I'll just go ahead and kill that pretty blonde of yours too."

Walker found enough strength to reach up and grab Mark's leg. But Mark easily stomped down on it, pinning it with his boot. Mark moved the barrel of his shotgun closer to Walker's head.

"Last chance. You don't tell me, I pull the trigger."

Just as Walker was mustering the strength to tell Mark where he could shove that shotgun, he saw Mark's head whip around behind him. Then all hell broke loose. Mark was too busy firing on someone toward the back of the church to worry about Walker. And though it was like pulling himself out of quicksand, Walker managed to get himself to his feet where he ducked down, ran four steps, and dove behind a row of church pews.

When Walker raised up, Mark had been backed up to the middle of the chapel. He was laying down rounds from his automatic rifle, firing toward the back door. Walker looked down and noticed that the first thing Mark must have done was take his weapons. He was weapons-naked, watching a gunfight.

Mark had two other men with him. They were firing at the front door. Walker didn't know what was going on. He had no idea who Mark and Vasquez's men could be shooting at. Since he didn't have a weapon, he stayed low, then pulled out his phone. He was hoping maybe he could find some answers there, or at least a message from Jon letting him know they made it out safe.

His phone had quite a few notifications, but he tapped on the last one that was from Jon: *It's Taylor. We're okay. I'm having the FBI track your phone so a team can come and help you. Please stay safe! Just get away from those men!*

The shooting stopped. The last few rounds Walker heard were from a pistol. Mark must have run out of ammo. When Walker looked up, the other men with Mark were either gone, or dead. Either way, it was just Mark standing in the middle of the chapel, all by himself, and he was holding a knife. And he was looking for Walker.

"Just us now, Walker. None of your FBI friends left to help you. This is your chance to learn what *real* fighting is. Not some no combat, sissy shit they teach you on some padded mats somewhere in Suburb, USA. Where they let you win to boost your confidence. I won't let you win."

Walker stood. "You won't have a choice."

Mark turned to face Walker. Walker stepped out into the open space just in front of the stairs to the podium.

"Seems like you wouldn't need that knife if you were as tough as you say you are."

Mark smiled. "There are no rules in a street fight, Walker. You're about to find that out."

Mark began walking toward him. Walker clenched and unclenched his fists. He had no idea how many fires Mark had been through in his life. Probably a lot. But few men had been burning since they were just a child the way that Walker had. And Mark was about to feel every spark. If one man was all he needed to get past to get himself free to go get Taylor, it would be the best odds he'd had all day.

So he hoped.

CHAPTER THIRTY-THREE

Mark stalked forward. Step one was to separate Mark and his knife. There were no other missions until that one was accomplished. Mark was doing the right thing, he wasn't sticking the knife straight out like a housewife fighting off a burglar in the kitchen, he had the top of the blade tucked along the underside of his forearm. Impossible for someone without knife skills to get to without getting cut.

Mark raised his hands up like a boxer would in a fist fight. His right hand was really going to sting if it landed. Walker had to isolate that arm. Mark came forward with a jab. Walker put his hands up, ready to defend. Two more jabs from Mark. He was controlled. He wasn't letting his emotions make him overextend like most amateurs would. Walker would have to wait for a mistake.

Mark jabbed again and Walker saw his opening. If he could place a perfectly timed kick to the left kidney, Mark would have to react, giving Walker a chance to advance. No matter how tough someone was, if it was a hard enough blow to the kidney, or the liver, they were going down.

Mark circled to his left, right into the power of Walker's

right kick. When Mark jabbed, Walker twisted his hips and put the toe of his shoe just under the floating ribs around the back of Mark's side. He grunted and dropped to his knee. Walker took advantage. He dove down, putting his head on Mark's right side, under his arm. As he drove forward, Mark landed on his back and Walker slid both arms to the wrist of Mark's knife hand, bending it down, forcing the blade into Mark's own forearm. He had no choice but to let go. The knife dropped to the hardwood.

Mark recovered quickly, taking advantage of Walker having no available arms to balance himself, so he lifted Walker up and tossed him down the aisle. Both men stood at the same time, hands in ready position, a little more respect in Mark's eyes now. Walker knew he had him.

This time Walker moved forward. Mark kicked but Walker raised his leg to check it as he came over the top with a straight right hand. Walker's knuckle glanced off of Mark's ear, but it was enough to push him back. Walker followed with a jab, cross, left hook combo. Only the hook landed, and it was a little high, catching Mark in the ribs. Walker ate a jab on his way back because he hadn't kept his hands up. But he parried Mark's oncoming right hand, and because he was already ducked down from getting hit with the jab, he exploded with an uppercut, springing up like a jack in the box.

Mark's teeth rattled with the crunching blow. He fell straight down on his back. Walker jumped on top of him, straddling him in full mount. The fight was over before it started. Mark was not going to escape Walker's mount. Mark was able to block the first couple of elbows Walker threw, but the second Walker grabbed his throat with his left hand, Mark was forced to use both his hands to try and remove it. This left plenty of space for Walker's right elbow, which he pounded down on Mark's forehead.

Walker felt Mark go limp beneath him, but he woke right back up. Walker had already pulled his arm up for another blow when a nearby radio squawked twice. Walker held his position as a man's voice followed the squawk.

"Peterson?"

Mark and Walker looked at each other. Walker was about to throw when he heard the voice again. Walker could see the legs of a man lying just a couple of pews up. It must have been one of the FBI agents that Taylor called in to help, and that Mark shot dead.

"Peterson, this is Alberts. Agent Crenshaw just called in a pickup for her and two others. The Pointe Marina at Harbour Island in Tampa. I need you to get there if you're free. We've got a mess down here with this murder victim on the porch. Peterson? Do you copy? I'll try your cell."

Before Walker could feel happy about hearing that Taylor was safe, he heard a gunshot and felt a searing pain in his left shoulder. On instinct he dove forward and rolled over beneath the pews.

"Put your weapons down!"

Walker heard a man shout from behind him at the front door. He raised up just in time to watch Mark sprint for the back. The man who'd shot Walker was still holding out his pistol, waiving Mark on with his other hand.

"Freeze!" Walker heard behind him.

He put his hands up and was forced to watch Mark and his gunman disappear out the back door.

"They're getting away!" Walker shouted. "I'm with Taylor. She had you track my phone to get here!"

"What's your name?" the man said.

"Tom Walker. They're getting away!"

"This is the guy Agent Crenshaw had us track," the man said. "Go and move to the back," the man said to his team.

Then to Walker, "Stay right there, Walker. We will get them. Stay out of this!"

But Walker knew they wouldn't. A group of four men rushed down the right aisle toward the back exit. Walker turned and ran toward the front door, bending down to pick up the radio he'd heard a moment ago, and the fallen agent's pistol that lay beside it. Walker could see Mark and his man already in a vehicle in his mind's eye. And thanks to that radio on the dead FBI agent, Mark knew exactly where Taylor and Jon were going to dock. Walker had to either get word to Jon and Taylor, or he had to make sure the police, the FBI, or someone was there to help them when they tried to dock the boat. Because Mark would just kill them all.

Walker had come this far, he couldn't let that happen now. He pulled out his phone as he ran for the front entrance. Blood was running down his left arm. He tapped Jon's contact as he sprinted out into the rain. From the top of the stairs, he watched Mark go by in the passenger seat of a black pickup truck. As it fishtailed out onto Pasadena Avenue, Jon's phone just continued to ring. And ring. And ring.

CHAPTER THIRTY-FOUR

Jon needed to steer the boat to the left in order to avoid some extremely shallow water. However, the way the waves were moving, he was afraid it was going to really throw them. He tried his best to wait until the right moment, but he was no expert captain. He felt a tap on his shoulder and it was Taylor handing him his phone back.

"Were you able to get Walker some help?" Jon shouted over the noise.

"I think so!" Taylor said. "And I think there will be a team waiting for us when we—"

Jon reached for the phone, but he should have had both hands on the steering wheel. The boat rode a wave the wrong way and turned the wheel harder than he wanted. The bow crashed down and sent all three of them to the deck of the boat. Jon tried to get to his feet but another wave came and put him right back down. He looked over and Jax was holding on to Taylor. They were trying not to take too much of a beating. But they were.

Jon didn't know if he should shut down the engine or just keep plowing ahead. They didn't have that much farther to go, and he knew that Taylor's preference would be to keep moving. He finally got a hand on the captain's chair and pulled himself up to the steering wheel. The water had pulled them closer to shore than he wanted so he had to steer back out into the bay. There was only about a half mile of visibility with all the rain and sea-spray, but he thought he could see where he wanted to go out in the distance. The bay beating they were taking was finally about to come to an end.

Jon did he best to minimize the jarring ride over the next fifteen minutes. It was slow going, but they pushed through. Taylor and Jax were able to make it back to the seat. Jon was able to stay in his chair. His arms were exhausted from trying to keep himself up, and steer the boat at the same time. The water had calmed quite a bit since they'd moved into the channel. They were surrounded by land on both sides now. Just a couple minutes left to go.

They could have found a dock much sooner than going all the way to Pointe Marina, but Jon wanted to make sure they were far away from Mark, and from Vazquez's minions. Pointe Marina was a good spot too for being easy for an FBI team to get to them, but also easy to get lost in some of the buildings just in case something went wrong.

Jon felt a hand on his shoulder. "Mind if I see your phone again? To make sure my people are here waiting?"

Jon reached for his pockets, but when he found them empty he remembered the missed exchange he and Taylor had when they were all thrown to the deck.

"I never got it back from you when the wave hit," Jon said. A look of horror formed on Taylor's rain-soaked face.

Taylor began searching the deck for the phone. She walked up front, then made her way toward the back. But she couldn't find it. Jon looked back and watched her talking to Jax. Jax pulled out his phone, looked at it, then shook his head. Taylor pulled her phone out again, then slammed it on the deck. Clearly hers wasn't working either.

"It's okay!" Jon said. "We're here! Can you keep her steady while I get the bumpers?"

Taylor walked toward him and took the wheel.

"Just keep it in the middle," Jon said.

Taylor nodded. Up ahead on their right was a large marina. There were several massive boats docked out front of a restaurant called Jackson's Bistro. There was a slip beside one of the bigger yachts. The boats were moving quite a bit in the wind, but not bad enough that Jon couldn't slide the boat in close enough to jump and tie it off.

Jon showed Jax where the bumpers were beneath the seat cushions. They pulled four of them out.

"You know how to tie these off?" Jon said.

Jax nodded. "I got it."

Jon pointed to the two chrome cleats at the back of the port side. Jon was moving up to the bow to tie two off there. They didn't need any on the starboard side, he was going to pull it in parallel. When they finished, Jax met him back in the middle of the boat.

"I'm going to pull it in so the bumpers are facing the dock. It's going to be really hard for me. So, if you get close enough and can jump to the dock to tie off the back I'll do my best to keep the front close until Taylor can toss you the rope for the front. Sound good?"

"I got you," Jax said.

Jon turned to Taylor. "You think you can toss him the rope?"

Taylor nodded as she relinquished the wheel to Jon.

"This is going to be rough!," Jon said to both of them. "Don't worry about the boat, let's just tie off and get the hell out of here!"

They moved to their positions at the front and back of

the boat. Jon didn't see a team of anybody around waiting for them, but this was the dock side of the marina. Any cars would have to be parked on the other side of the marina mall. He pushed the throttle forward and they moved toward the dock. The rain was still heavy, and so was the wind, but the land around them had calmed the water to a dull roar.

Jon was not qualified for this kind of docking job. He just tried to keep in mind that he had to steer the boat with the stern as he was moving in. That's what his instructor had taught him just a couple of weeks ago. But that was a lot easier said than done when he had been practicing it. Even in calm water.

Jon moved in toward the dock. When he got close, he turned the wheel to the right, letting the stern move left. The waves were pushing him closer than he'd anticipated so he throttled forward a hair just to even it out. It went pretty good and Jax showed no fear in jumping off. Jon turned the wheel just a bit to straighten up and then cut the engine and took the key. He went running for the bow just as the bumper slammed the dock. Jax was still tying off so Jon jumped to the dock. His feet flew out from under him on the wet deck and he busted his ass. But he was okay.

He turned toward the boat as he stood and held out his hands. Taylor tossed him the rope and he tied off to the cleat. He finished at about the same time Jax had. They'd made it. Jon walked over to the boat and took Taylor by the hands, helping her off the boat. They were all beat up, soaked, and freezing, but they were alive.

They were also alone.

What they didn't know was that they should have been happy about that. Because they weren't going to like who was about to show up.

CHAPTER THIRTY-FIVE

Walker had almost wrecked three times since he'd taken one of the FBI's SUVs that they left running when they went inside the church. He was trying to do too many things at once. He was trying to keep up with Mark's truck, which he'd never caught up to after seeing it leave the church parking lot. So, he had to type in the Pointe Marina address into the GPS. At the same time, he was still trying to get Jon or Taylor to answer their phones to warn them, but had no luck there. All while doing his best to stop the bleeding coming from the bullet hole in his shoulder.

Walker found a shirt in the back seat and had been using it as a towel to try to sop up his leaking blood. When he felt for the wounds, there was a hole on both sides. Painful, but no bullet inside. It had gone right through his deltoid muscle. All that going on, and the rain was still coming down, and he'd nearly clipped two cars and a parked bus as he was trying to turn, following the GPS's directions.

He had just turned off of Selmon Expressway and made a right onto S. Harbour Island Drive. He was close. And while he couldn't have been more than a couple of minutes behind

Mark's truck, he had no idea when Jon's boat would be getting to the marina. All he knew was that a couple of minutes could easily be the difference between life and death. So he had to hurry.

As he crossed over onto the small island, Pointe Marina came into view. It was sitting on what looked to be the point of the triangle shaped island. He didn't see any movement out on the dock, but only the side of the point facing him was visible. The other side, closer to the bay, would be where Jon's boat would be coming in from. So they could be there right now. And so could Mark.

As he came off the bridge, his stomach dropped. The truck Mark was in was parked out front of the marina. There were other cars, because the marina was attached to a Westin hotel, but the truck wasn't in a space, just pulled right up to the front. Walker turned his SUV into the parking lot and pulled right up behind it. There was a Starbucks just to the left of the marina entrance, but the lights were out. No one was getting out in this weather, and there was a good chance that the power had already gone out. He glanced around at the condos that surrounded the area and didn't see a light on.

The clouds were dark enough above to make it seem like night was closing in, but it was only around five o'clock in the evening. There was no movement in Mark's truck so Walker got out and moved toward the marina's entrance. It reminded him of a something more like a shopping mall. It was a large two story building filled with restaurants, boat rentals, and other office space on the second floor. Walker didn't know where to start so he jogged for the Jackson's Bistro entrance.

A woman's scream broke through the wind. It sounded like it was on the dock side of the marina. It had to be Taylor.

Walker sprinted through the restaurant entrance. It was

dark, but he could see the light coming in from the patio at the back of the restaurant.

"Can I help you sir?" a woman said as he dodged a dining table.

"Call the police! There's been a shooting!" he shouted.

Walker didn't look over to see her reaction. He sprinted out onto the patio, then over toward the boats. The wind was smacking him in the face with rain. He looked down the dock toward the Westin and saw two men running. He ran around the turn that went left. There he could see up in front of the two men, closer to the hotel, and he watched as the back of someone disappeared inside.

Walker wanted to shoot. But he couldn't be sure who he was shooting at. He wanted to shout, but if it was Mark and his gunman, he didn't want to let them know he was there. So he ran after them, the gun he took from the FBI agent in his hand, down by his side.

The two figures entered the Westin on the left. The boats on the right side on the water were rocking steadily where they were docked. Walker wasn't far behind the men and he made it to the entrance. It was too dark to see anything inside so he opened the door and moved in.

The air conditioning gave him a chill. He nearly knocked down a couple moving to get a look at the storm through the glass door he'd just come through.

"Sorry," he said. "Did you see two other guys in a hurry?"

"That way," the lady said as she pointed.

Gun shots rang out from the direction she'd just motioned toward. Walker sprinted down a hallway, doors to rooms on both sides. Then it opened up into the main lobby. The check-in counter was on the right and two men were standing on the left side, pointing guns in that direction. There was a man lying on the floor in front of one of the check-in counters. He was black, and it looked an awful lot like the navy blue EMT jacket that Jax was wearing.

Walker raised his gun and shot the man standing in front of Mark. Mark spun and Walker dove as bullets came his way. The few people in the lobby were screaming. Walker was lying behind an art deco chair that didn't have a lot coverage. All he could think about was Jax, and whether or not Taylor had already suffered the same fate. The gunshots stopped and Walker raised up. Mark was gone.

A woman in the corner, off to Walker's left, pointed to a door at the opposite side of the lobby. Walker sprinted over to Jax. He didn't want to move him.

"Call for some help, please!" Walker shouted. "The police, an ambulance, call everyone and then get the hell out of here!"

Walker saw a woman get on her phone so he moved for the door he was told Mark went through. Before he could cross the threshold more gunshots came. Then sirens. Someone must have called the police as soon as they saw Mark run in with a gun. Mark's time was running out. But Walker wanted to seal his fate before there was any chance of Vasquez's money getting him out of trouble with the law. He knew that if Mark died here, Vasquez would just cut his losses and move on. That's what had to happen.

Walker ran through the door and there were dozens of chairs lined up in a row, a large projector screen at the far end. It was an auditorium set up for a conference. At the far end, to the left of the massive screen he saw Mark running through a door. He raised his gun and fired twice but Mark was already through. He heard screams and gasps from the lobby behind him. And the screeching tires and sirens of police just outside.

Walker ran for the back of the room, and with each step it became darker. The only reason he was able to see Mark a moment ago was because his white shirt reflected the light coming in from the lobby doors. Now it was just black.

"I know you're in here, Jon," Mark's voice made it out into the conference room. "Say something right now and I'll let the woman go."

Walker felt around with his hands and found the doorway. Whatever light that had made it to the doorway, stopped before it got in the room. It was pitch black. With the power being out, and no windows, there was no way someone could be seen inside. Walker thought about turning on his phone light, but if he shined it on the wrong spot and exposed Jon and Taylor, Mark would easily be able to shoot them. So he stepped inside the darkness.

The first thing he did was nearly trip over a table that was only a couple of steps in. He decided to duck down behind it and draw Mark's attention.

"There's no way out of this for you, Mark. I'm here, the police are here, it's over. You're either walking out of here in handcuffs, or not walking out at all."

A couple of shots came his way from the left corner of the room. He saw the muzzle flash and returned fire. He heard Mark grunt. He'd actually hit him.

"You dumb son of a bitch, Walker. Whatever happens here, whether you save Jon, or you kill me, it doesn't matter. Vasquez and his men will find you."

Walker crouched as he felt for another table a few feet down. "No he won't. You're nothing to him. You were something to Jon. Jon would have fought for you. Vasquez will just mark you off his payroll list."

"Bullshit!" Mark shouted.

A couple more shots came Walker's way, one ricocheting off the table. Then the strangest thing happened. They say that when one of your senses is taken away, your others become heightened. For a second he thought it was wishful thinking, but then it was just too strong to deny. He could smell Taylor's perfume. It was faint, but he knew that smell. He'd made love to it more than once, and it was imprinted on his brain. He moved quickly toward it.

"Come on, Walker. This is your only chance before the police get their shot. And you know they're not trained well enough for me."

Walker held out his hands as he moved. He felt a table, his hand ran across multiple chairs, but then it landed on something stringy and wet. Then he felt two arms wrap around him just as the smell of Taylor's perfume really came in strong.

"Walker!" Mark shouted.

Two more gunshots.

Walker squeezed Taylor close. He could feel her heart thudding. He felt for Jon and found his arm. He pulled him in and made sure he had a hold of Taylor. Then he moved his mouth down to her ear.

Walker whispered. "Run toward the light, and don't stop until you both are safe. On three, start running."

Walker let go of her and moved past her. He jogged down the length of the room as he counted to three in his head. When he heard Jon and Taylor running for the door, he opened fire in the corner where he last saw the gunshots coming from. But Mark had moved, just like Walker had, and Walker felt two hands wrap around his gun hand while a kick swept him off his feet. Walker's gun fell to the floor at the same time he did. And as soon as Walker hit the carpet, he felt Mark fall on top of him, then something hard crashed down on his temple.

Then there was nothing.

CHAPTER THIRTY-SIX

A sharp pain stabbed at Walker's head. The second he woke up he was confused because everything was black. He moved his head to the left to try and see and when he did it helped Mark's next punch to merely graze his ear. Everything came flooding back to Walker and he reached up, wrapping his arms around Mark. He pulled him down close so Mark couldn't raise up for another punch.

"I'm gonna kill you, you son of a bitch!" Mark said.

Walker took a deep breath and let it out slow as he held Mark. In a blink, Walker moved both hands to Mark's hips, shoved hard, and pulled his knees up to his chest. Mark fell back down on him but this time Walker's legs were free and he wrapped them around Mark's lower back as he once again pulled him close. Walker then took his time. Like a boa constrictor, he squeezed tight, leaving Mark without an inch of wiggle room. Mark was fighting it, and breathing heavy in Walker's ear. But he wasn't properly fighting it.

Walker then bucked his hips and pushed Mark's upper body up and over his head. He was free. But Mark was too. And he could hear Mark take off running just as soon as he got to his feet. Walker didn't have time to feel for his gun on the floor. He just started moving toward the light coming in through the door. He heard Mark stumble over a chair, then watched him run through the door. Walker sprinted after him.

Instead of going back in the direction of the lobby, Mark had gone left.

"Freeze!" a man screamed from the direction of the lobby. "Don't move!"

Walker turned left and followed Mark who'd already opened and run through another door on the other side of the projector screen. He knew where Mark was going. With the police outside, and Walker in there, his only way of having a chance to escape was the weather. If he could get on one of the boats and make it out into the water, they couldn't follow him. And he just might be able to get away.

Walker rushed through the door that led to a hallway. There was a light at the far end, but it was dark in between. But he heard a woman tell someone to "watch it!", so he knew he was in the right place. He sprinted down the hallway, jumping an overturned housekeeping cart. The same woman said something to Walker as he ran by but he didn't catch what it was. Up ahead, the door letting in the light had a shadow in front of it, and then it was open. Just before he got to the door he heard an entirely different sort of siren. One he'd only heard on television or in the movies, but he knew what it was immediately. It was coming from off in the distance. The wind carrying the sound from the beaches. What they thought was just going to be a tropical storm must have changed. Sirens meant mandatory evacuations.

A hurricane was coming.

When Walker made it outside the hotel, the rain was gone. The wind was stronger than ever, and over by the coast, the clouds were turning into something wicked. But

Walker couldn't let that distract him. He had to do the only thing that would keep him from having even more people to hide from in his life, and keep Taylor and Jon safe for good. Something he never would want to do because he has so much respect for the military. But sometimes people give a man no choice. There was no other option.

He had to kill the Green Beret.

Walker scanned the area. No one was outside on the water side of the hotel. That's why it was easy to see Mark climbing onto the side of a boat. Walker raced forward. Hesitation now might mean Mark's escape. As he approached the boat, he heard it start up. Walker jumped over the boat's rail and landed on top of Mark. They both went down to the deck. For the first time in a while Walker felt the hole in his shoulder fill with a burning flame.

Mark reached back for the cooler that was lying near by. Walker was trying to secure position so his hands were occupied and Mark hit him over the head with it. Walker fell onto his back. Mark scrambled, keeping the cooler in his hand and came forward. Walker kicked up into his groin and Mark dropped the cooler as he dropped to his knees. Walker threw a right hand as he raised up and broke Mark's nose. Blood exploded from his nostrils. It was Mark's turn to fall to his back.

Walker advanced. The sirens still wailed in the distance. The wind was getting stronger, and colder by the second. Walker mounted Mark and brought an elbow down so hard that the smack echoed inside the fiberglass boat. Mark was unconscious. Walker brought down another elbow, this one carried with it the fury being on top of the man who tried to kill Taylor. It caved in Mark's cheekbone. He raised up for another blow when he heard a man shout from the dock.

"Freeze! Don't make another move!"

Walker looked over and a police officer was pointing a

gun at him. He looked down at Mark. He was unconscious, battered, and bloodied, but he wasn't dead. The job wasn't finished. Peace of mind would never come if he didn't end it for good right then and there. He knew from experience because even though Maxwell Solutions—the clandestine group that made him a killer—thought Walker was dead, he still was constantly looking over his shoulder. Why? Because Maxwell Solutions wasn't dead. Loose ends make for sleepless nights.

Walker was through with loose ends. He was going to tie this one off with Mark, then he was going to finish things with Maxwell Solutions once and for all. Things had never been clearer. But right then he was staring down the barrel of an officer's gun. If he hit Mark one more time, he believed the officer would shoot him.

Walker raised both hands to the sky. Then he nodded to the officer. The officer touched his shoulder radio, "Suspect is at the docks behind the Westin. Requesting backup. I have him at gunpoint, but requesting backup."

Before the officer could get his second hand back in firing position, Walker reached down and picked Mark up.

"Freeze I said!" the officer shouted.

However, Walker had already pulled Mark up and was holding him between himself and the officer—using him as a shield. Then he took two steps back toward the starboard side rail of the boat.

"Don't move! I said don't move!"

But Walker did. He sat his butt down on the rail, then pitched backward like a scuba diver entering the water. He had his hands locked together, wrapped around Mark in a bear hug. The two of them went headfirst into the water.

"Let him go!" the officer shouted.

There was nothing left for the officer to do. He'd done his job, now it was time for Walker to do his. When they hit the water, Walker adjusted his legs in a reverse triangle choke around Mark's neck. There was no way he could get loose. Walker swam over to the side of the boat, took a deep breath, and pulled himself underneath the boat, ensuring that the officer—even if he climbed onto the boat—couldn't get an angle on him to shoot.

Walker let everything relax except for the squeeze of his legs around Mark. The first thing that flashed in his mind as he held Mark under was Taylor's face. Then Jon and Walker laughing at the gun range. Then, he saw Karen Maxwell. The head of Maxwell Solutions, and the reason Walker had never truly felt free. All because she turned on him, and then tried to erase him. She had been responsible for killing more perfectly good men and women than maybe any other person doing jobs for the US government. She had to be stopped. For Walker's sake, and for the sake of many other men and women who were doing their job in the name of their beloved country.

Mark didn't thrash. He was still unconscious from Walker's shots on the boat. He was already dead at that point, but Walker didn't want to take any more chances. As he held himself under the boat, and Mark under the water, he thought of how strange the human mind can be. How moments of clarity, like the one Walker had been wrestling with since the day Karen Maxwell sent three men to kill him in his hometown in Kentucky, could come at a time of such chaos. But as long as he could leave Tampa without being thrown in jail, his next trip was going to be Washington D.C. To take his freedom for the first time in his life.

Walker let go of Mark. He swam a few feet out away from the boat and put his hands in the air as he kicked his legs in the water.

"I surrender!" he shouted.

The officer came running over to the rail of the boat, still pointing his gun. His eyes were searching the water for Mark.

"He's dead, officer," Walker said as he nodded toward the bow of the boat. "Floating right over there."

Several other officers, and plain clothed men and women with guns ran up to the edge of the dock.

The nightmare was over.

CHAPTER THIRTY-SEVEN

As a group of police officers fished Mark's body out of the bay, Walker pulled himself out of the water to at least four guns held on him. He put his hands up when asked, dropped to his knees too, and held out his hands. Since this was the first time he'd been arrested since he'd strangled his foster father to death when he was fifteen, he couldn't help but have a few flashbacks. None of them were pleasant.

The decision he made that day to make his foster father stop hitting Kim for good changed the course of his life forever. It was the reason he'd become a killer, and ultimately, it was the reason the Tampa Bay Police Department was walking him soaking wet and handcuffed back to a squad car at the front of the hotel.

The police officer who'd tried to save Mark from Walker looked at Walker like he was some sort of demon. He supposed he was to a lot of people. One of the last things a decent, moral, God-fearing human being could ever fathom was taking another person's life. Walker didn't even think twice. He wasn't sure what that said about him. But any way he looked at it, it probably wasn't good.

The hurricane warning sirens had stopped. Walker could see the storm moving North, just as the weather people had predicted. It must have been a close call though for someone to order the sirens. The wind had subsided and the rain held itself to a steady sprinkle.

They took Walker through the hotel. His wrists were uncomfortable, but at least they'd cuffed him in the front. He felt like a zoo animal being paraded onto one of the late night talk shows. "Here we have the *humanous murderous*," the zoo keeper would tell the audience. "Just look at the way he kills without remorse."

The hotel was still dark. People were poking their heads out of their rooms to see the show.

"Hey," a woman said when they passed. "That was the good guy. Why are you arresting him?"

Walker just kept his head down. He knew there was no argument to be made at the moment. The police had literally just watched a civilian drown someone to death. They were going to have to do their due diligence. They made it into the lobby, Walker's heart sank when he saw Jax being zipped into a body bag. Another life ended because of the way Walker was living his.

Walker glanced over where he'd shot Mark's gunman—the man who'd shot Walker—but they must have already taken him out in a bag. The two officers holding Walker by his arms walked him out front. That's when he saw Taylor. As soon as she saw him in handcuffs her worried look turned to anger. She came charging over to them.

"You let him go right now. This man is a hero, not a criminal."

"Ma'am, please step aside," one of the officers said.

Taylor pulled her FBI credentials and held them up. "I'm not asking, officer. Un-cuff him. I'll take him into custody."

The officers stopped. "Ma'am, you know I can't do that.

We just watched him murder someone, and until it gets sorted out by people way above my pay grade, I have to take him into custody. You can make your case with the sheriff down at the station."

When she knew she wasn't going to get her mission accomplished with the officers, she shifted focus to Walker. "Don't worry, I will get this taken care of. You won't spend a night in jail." Then she looked at his shoulder. "You're bleeding," then to the officer, "He's bleeding. Get an ambulance for him right now."

"His life isn't in danger ma'am. We've been instructed that he will be medically seen to at the station. Now please, just step aside."

They were at the patrol car.

Taylor looked at Walker. "I'll follow you to the station. I'll be right there. I'll get this taken care of."

Walker gave a faltering smile and a nod. He believed her, he was just tired. It was coming over him in a wave of exhaustion. The officers opened the back door of the police cruiser. Taylor stepped aside.

"Thank you, Tom."

He looked up at her after they sat him inside. Though she'd seen one hell of a twenty-four hours, she still looked beautiful. He smiled.

"Thank you," she said again.

The officer shut the car door. Taylor tapped on the window, "I'll be right behind you!"

Then the car pulled away. The two officers turned around in their seats to look at Walker, the driver said, "You really the good guy?"

"Depends who you ask, I suppose," Walker said.

The two of them laughed and then turned around. The female officer said, "Well that FBI lady sure thinks so. Guess you've got that going for you."

"Guess I do," Walker said.

They pulled out of the Westin parking lot and turned left onto S. Harbour Island Drive.

"What happened to the storm?" Walker said.

"Hung around longer than they thought, that's why they blew the sirens," the female officer said. "But it went North of here. Slowed down quite a bit at the end. I think it won't be too bad."

"That's good."

Walker saw the female officer lean forward and look at the sideview mirror. "That FBI lady wasn't kidding. She's rolling right behind us." She turned and looked over her shoulder at Walker. "That's got to make you feel good, right?"

Walker smiled.

She looked over at the driver. "Maybe he's not the bad guy."

The driver shrugged. "Maybe not."

They crossed over the water and onto the mainland. Walker noticed that the traffic was a little heavier than when he'd driven there earlier.

The driver looked at Walker in the rearview mirror. "So, if you're not the bad guy, then who the hell is?"

The police car was coming to an intersection. The light was green so the officer was rolling right through. Walker looked left just in time to see the front end of the black pickup truck that was racing toward them, and it smashed right into the driver's side of the police cruiser, sending both vehicles crashing off the road.

CHAPTER THIRTY-EIGHT

Walker had the sensation that he was floating through the air like an astronaut in space. Zero gravity. It was the sound that first brought him back to reality. Twisting metal, breaking glass, the female officer screaming as the police cruiser rolled over and over again.

Then there was the pain. First his left shoulder that had already been badly injured. It felt like it was being pounded with a baseball bat equipped with metal spikes. Next, his head smashed into the window beside him, then his wrists got twisted up in the handcuffs, digging deep enough into his skin to bring blood. Finally, it all came to a skidding halt.

The female officer was groaning in pain. Which was a good sign. The driver was lifeless, his head was bent oddly as he crunched into the roof of the car. It took Walker a second before he realized the car was upside down. He was so disoriented. The cruiser's engine was hissing. Walker could smell oil and gasoline. He needed to pull it together.

He blinked a few heavy blinks, trying to pull reality out of something so surreal. He was lying on his good shoulder, his knees up near his chin. Among all the swirling sounds, pains, and emotions, his mind's eye showed him the front of the black pickup truck that he saw just before it hit the police car.

Walker's eyes opened wide. *It wasn't an accident*, his mind shouted at him.

"It wasn't an accident," Walker said as he went into a coughing fit. Then he started to kick the partition that separated him from the officers. "Wake up! This wasn't an accident. Do you hear me? Wake up!"

He searched desperately for a way to get out of the car on his own, but it was specifically designed so that he couldn't. The female officer groaned again.

"Please wake up! You have to get me out of here. Wake up or we're both going to die!"

The officer groaned again, but then roused enough to speak. "What—what happened?"

"Someone is trying to kill us. This wasn't an accident!"

Finally she snapped to attention and her head whipped around to look for Walker. "Wait, what?"

Walker evened out his tone. "They're trying to kill me. And they'll kill you too. You have to—"

Gunshots rang out just outside the cruiser.

"Get me out of here!"

Finally the officer opened her door and rolled outside. Three more gunshots broke the silence. Walker's door opened and he rolled out onto the ground.

"Un-cuff me!" he whisper-shouted. "Hurry!"

The officer fumbled in her pocket but didn't find the keys at first.

"Walker, look out!" Taylor's voice rose above the fray. Followed by several more gunshots.

That's when the man who shot Walker in the chapel—the man Walker shot twice in the hotel lobby—walked around the front of the car. His white shirt was covered in blood where Walker had shot him. No wonder Walker hadn't seen him lying in the hotel lobby in a body bag like Jax had been. He wasn't dead.

The officer looked up, astonished, and fumbled for her gun, but it was too late. The gunman already had a shotgun held on her. As Walker was scurrying to his feet, half the officers face blew back onto him. The man turned the gun on Walker but he was too slow. Walker dove under the shotgun and put his shoulder into the gunman's thigh. They both went down but Walker jumped on him, using both hands to crawl into position.

If his hands would have been cuffed behind his back, Walker would have been dead.

Instead, he straddled the gunman. His brown eyes looked up at Walker as if he knew what was coming, and was okay with it. Walker clasped his hands and hammered down on the gunman's head. It didn't knock him out, so the man squirmed until he was on his stomach. That would be his final mistake.

Walker wrapped the small length of chain between his handcuffs around the man's neck. He pulled hard, and rolled over as he did it. Now the man's back was resting on Walker's stomach. Walker wrapped his legs around the man to hold him in position. There was no escape for him.

Taylor and Jon came running up by the overturned police cruiser, just as Walker was pushing up with his hips and pulling down with his wrists.

"Terry?" Jon said.

Walker knew then that Terry was one of Mark's long-time guys. That's why he came back for Walker. Loyal to a fault.

"Tom, you can let go," Taylor said.

But he couldn't. Or, he wouldn't. Not till it was finished. Terry wasn't fighting Walker. Walker was choking him so hard that Terry couldn't even make a sound.

"Walker?"

He looked over at Taylor while he continued to choke Terry. With the blood and brains of the office plastered all over him, he couldn't imagine what he looked like to her. But it couldn't have been good, because Jon took her by the arm and turned her away.

Two men ran up. They looked like they might be FBI. They shouted at Walker and rushed down to rip Terry from his grasp. Walker didn't fight them. He knew they were too late. Terry was dead this time.

That was the last bit of energy that Walker had to give. He rolled over on his stomach, resting his forehead on his right forearm. Exhausted. Taylor ran over, bent down beside him, and placed her hand on his back.

"Are you—"

"It's not my blood," he managed. "Well, not all of it."

"Just sit tight, we have an ambulance coming right now."

He wasn't sure he had a choice. He couldn't really move. The next thing he knew a couple of EMT's were helping him on a stretcher. It made him think of Jax. It made him sad. He wondered if the man who risked his life for them had a family. Maybe he could find out and help them somehow.

Just as they were about to shut the doors to the ambulance, Taylor fought her way through the small crowd that had gathered. The EMT stopped her and told her family only. Taylor told her to just try and keep her from getting in that ambulance. The EMT just let her go. Walker couldn't help but smile. She grabbed a towel that was sitting on a shelf, then sat in the seat beside him. She began wiping some of the blood off of his face as she held his hand. She had put her hair up in a ponytail and was wearing a towel around her shoulders. The ambulance door was shutting, but then it stopped again.

"Just give me a couple seconds. I promise that's it and I'll go."

"It's not like anyone is listening to me anyway," the EMT said.

Jon hopped up in the ambulance. He walked over to Walker's right side, shaking his head. "You don't look so hot." Jon was smiling.

"You should see the other guy," Walker joked.

Jon's face went solemn. "About that. I'm real sorry, Walker."

Walker tried to sit up, but Taylor placed her hand on his chest. "Just relax."

"I'm sorry about your son, Jon."

"I made this damn mess, Walker. I'm just sorry for all the hurt it caused. I'll let you get to the hospital, I just had to jump in here and say it. I might not see you for a while."

Walker thought he knew what Jon meant, that he was going to do some prison time, but Walker just kept it to himself.

"Walker nodded. "Take care, Jon."

Jon looked at Taylor. "I know I said it already, Agent Crenshaw, but again . . . I'm sorry."

Taylor smiled. Jon turned and jumped down out of the ambulance. Police were there waiting on him.

"I think I can help reduce what they're going to want to charge him with. Especially when he cooperates about Javier Vasquez."

"He's a good man who was trapped in a bad situation," Walker said.

Taylor patted his hand. "Sounds like somebody else I know." She leaned down and gave him a long kiss on the forehead. "Thank you for risking your life for me. I know you're going to say it's what you do, but it isn't what you had to do, and I'm here, alive, because of you."

Walker squeezed her hand. "You can make it up to me later."

He tried to laugh with Taylor, but it hurt in more than one place, so he quit. The ambulance door shut, and a few seconds later they were on their way to the hospital.

"Hell of a three days," Walker said.

Taylor caressed his jaw. "Hell of a three days."

CHAPTER THIRTY-NINE

Two Weeks Later

Nashville, Tennessee

The sun was bright at high noon over Broadway in Nashville, Tennessee. Walker had been recovering for the last couple of weeks in Kentucky while Taylor was wrapping things up with Jon's whole debacle. She promised to get into the details, but not before she had her first drink.

The two of them had stayed in close contact during that time. Walker finally knew what it was like to be a Gen Z falling in love. There weren't many times that they went more than an hour without a text or a call. Usually just a fun message filled with emoji's, or sharing a funny meme one of them had found. They chose to meet in Nashville because it was an easy drive for Walker, and an easy flight for Taylor from Tampa.

They both had healed well from their war wounds. They

shared pictures as their injuries progressed. Walker asked for a couple of pictures that didn't involve injuries. Taylor was kind enough to oblige. Both of them were very much looking forward to seeing each other again. Taylor told him just to book one room. He wasn't the type to argue.

Walker left a day early for Nashville. He took the very long way around and stopped off in Soddy Daisy to see his buddy Tim Lawson. They laid by the lake and drank themselves silly for a day. It was fantastic.

Walker told Tim about Jax, the EMT who saved his and Taylor's life. Walker had been able to get in contact with the family Jax had left behind. He'd told them about how their husband, and father, had been a hero. The military was picking up the tab for the funeral, but Walker set up college funds for Jax's son and daughter. He was going to make sure they at least had that much. Walker didn't know if he was doing it for Jax, Jax's family, or for his own conscience. Either way, he figured he was doing something good.

"Quite the crowd here today," Taylor said. "It's been a long time since I've been here. It's completely different."

"It is . . . different," Walker said.

Walker watched as a group of bridesmaids went by. They were all wearing a black sash. Four of the sashes said "Bad Influence" in white. One said, "Maid of Dishonor", and the bride came through with a tiara, and a whites sash with gold writing that said, "Wife of the Party."

Taylor and Walker looked at each other and laughed.

They were on the rooftop patio at Jason Aldean's Kitchen and Rooftop Bar. There was a live band playing inside. The sound easily carrying to the outdoor seating. Walker was sipping on a Buffalo Trace Bourbon and sweet tea. Taylor was having a margarita. He reached his glass over and clanked it against hers.

"I don't know what you've done," Walker said. "But you look even better than the last time I saw you."

"Yeah? Not being chased by killers usually helps."

"Been a slow couple weeks then."

They laughed.

"I missed you, Tom."

"I missed you, too."

All Walker really wanted to do was finish his drink in one swallow and take her to the hotel. She said she wanted the same earlier, but thought the tease of an afternoon out first would be fun. Fun isn't the word Walker would use. But he was managing.

"All right," Walker said. "How bad is it for Jon?"

She drank. "You know I can't speak on the specifics, but lets just say that he's not in jail at this moment. And he's decided to cooperate, so if something comes of that, he won't see time at all."

Walker, as much as any American, had a sense of justice. And he was sure that for the wrong's Jon had done, he should have to pay. Though, losing a son, no matter how much of a loser, would be punishment enough in Walker's eyes. But, he understood why Jon should be in trouble. And even though he caused Walker a lot of trouble, Walker still hoped he could find a way to stay out of prison.

"I hope he can get you something that will give him a second chance."

She nodded. "Me too. I like Jon. Crazy to think what a few bad decisions can lead to. Good person or not."

"It really is."

The bridal party just got delivered a tray of shots. If there was a sportsbook at Aldean's letting patrons wager on whether or not a particular group would see midnight, Walker would bet a healthy sum that these ladies would not. The "Maid of Dishonor" would make sure of that.

"I do not miss those days," Taylor said looking on while the bridal party bit limes to chase their tequila.

"Pretty sure I remember you buying us shots at Caddy's. You sure you're not a "Maid of Dishonor" yourself?"

Taylor nearly spit out her margarita. "I have definitely been known to stir the pot once in a while. But that's been a while."

"I wouldn't mind seeing Party Taylor."

"Oh, yes. Yes you very much *would* mind. Party Taylor is fun for a while, but there's always a moment where it takes a turn."

"Hmm," Walker laughed. "I'm not convinced. I think I'm going to go grab us a couple of shots."

Taylor gave him the side eye with a smile. Then she shrugged, closed her eyes, and turned her face toward the sun. "It does feel like a good day for a little day buzz."

Walker stood from the table. "Is there ever a day that isn't good for a little day buzz?"

"Not on a day off."

Walker leaned in for a kiss. He went to back away but she held him close and kept his lips a little longer.

"Whew," she said. "Drinks, then the hotel. Okay hot stuff?"

Walker gave her a salute and she smacked him on his ass as he walked away. It felt more like he was floating away he was in such a good mood. When he moved inside the music went up a few decibels. The place was packed. Everyone was laughing and having a good time. It was just a great day.

Walker saddled up to the bar. A cute brunette came over —couldn't have been a day over twenty-one—tipped her cowgirl hat and asked him what he was having. Her nametag said Stacey.

"Two shots of tequila with a lime."

She smiled, "Time to make it a party?"

"Why not?" Walker said.

"Indeed."

She walked away and poured the shots. Walker looked back but he didn't see Taylor sitting at their table. Normally, it wouldn't have even registered to him. But after what they'd gone through just a couple weeks ago, he'd be lying if he said it didn't immediately put him on edge.

Walker had his card out when Stacey came back.

"Keep it open?" she said.

"You can close it."

She took the card, swiped it, and handed it back. Then she handed him the pen and a receipt. He signed it and slipped it back to her.

"Me and the girls noticed you two on your way in. Gorgeous couple," Stacey winked.

Walker held up the shots. "Thank you. And thanks for the drinks."

When he walked away from the bar, Taylor still wasn't in her seat. A jolt of anxiety shot through him. He was so focused on their table that he almost ran over a waitress going by with a tray of food. He finally reached the patio when he looked to his left and there she was, taking pictures for the bridal party.

Walker breathed a sigh of relief. He felt stupid. It was also in that moment that he realized just how much he liked Taylor. She looked over, he held up the shots, and a huge smile grew across her face. She walked back over and wrapped her arms around him.

"You were gone too long," she said as she went onto her toes for a long kiss. "Those girls are fun, but I doubt they'll see much nightlife tonight. They're already wild."

Walker could hear Taylor speaking, but none of what she said registered. The next thing he knew, the shots of tequila he was holding shattered on the ground at his feet.

"Tom?" Taylor turned and grasped his arm. "What is it? What's wrong?"

Walker flashed back to the moment he had beneath the boat when he was holding Mark underwater to drown him just outside of the Westin hotel. Particularly, the part where he'd made up his mind that he was going to tie off all the loose ends in his life, including the one at Maxwell Solutions, the keeper of his freedom. The same reason why he had anxiety at the bar a moment ago when he hadn't seen Taylor at their table. The secret government program still had a hold on him, and it was because the head of the group that tried to kill him, was still breathing.

His time on the run was over. And just in case he wasn't going to follow his intuition to take down Maxwell Solutions, the Universe had made it so he couldn't miss it. In fact, it was staring him right in the face. As he looked down at the white piece of paper sitting on the table just in front of his chair, he understood that someone from Maxwell Solutions had given him a chance to fight. They'd left him a message, and now his future was written right in front of him, in stark black ink:

Dear Tom Walker, Karen Maxwell knows you're alive.

DELIVERANCE
by
Bradley Wright
Preorder book four
in the Tom Walker series today!

DELIVERANCE
by
Bradley Wright
Book four in the Tom Walker
series will be available in 2024!

ACKNOWLEDGMENTS

First and foremost, I want to thank you, the reader. I love what I do, and no matter how many people help me along the way, none of it would be possible if you weren't turning the pages.

To my family and friends. Thank you for always being there with mountains of support. You all make it easy to dream, and those dreams are what make it into these books. Without you, no fun would be had, much less novels be written.

To my advanced reader team. You continue to help make everything I do better. You all have become friends, and I thank you for catching those last few sneaky typos, and always letting me know when something isn't good enough. Tom Walker appreciates you, and so do I.

Advanced team all-stars were Dbie Johnson, Brad Burdick, Jeff Javorski, Diane Carter, Karen Dimitrijevski, Camille Cihat, and Leslie Bryant. Thank you so much for the extra tender-loving care you gave to this story.

About the Author

Bradley Wright is the international bestselling author of espionage and mystery thrillers. BLIND PASS is his twenty-first novel. Bradley lives with his family in Lexington, Kentucky. He has always been a fan of great stories, whether it be a song, a movie, a novel, or a binge-worthy television series. Bradley loves interacting with readers on Facebook, Twitter, and via email.

Join the online family:
www.bradleywrightauthor.com
info@bradleywrightauthor.com

Printed in Great Britain
by Amazon